'Ambermere must be a unique property, if it can rouse such passionate commitment in you.' He paused. 'I wonder, in different circumstances, if you would ever have found the husband you are looking for, Julia Kendrick—a man so little a man he would deny his name and his birthright in subjection to your whim.'

Her voice sounded high and rather breathless. 'When you take Ambermere, you'll have done the worst you can. You have no power over me after that.'

'You don't think so?' Slowly he advanced on her, making her retreat until her back was pressed against the balustrade with no further physical withdrawal possible. 'But you are wrong, Julia Kendrick. Because if I take Ambermere, I shall also take you.'

KING OF
SWORDS

BY

SARA CRAVEN

MILLS & BOON LIMITED
ETON HOUSE   18-24 PARADISE ROAD
RICHMOND   SURREY   TW9 1SR

First published in Great Britain 1988
by Mills & Boon Limited

© Sara Craven 1988

Australian copyright 1988
Philippine copyright 1988
This edition 1988

ISBN 0 263 76086 3

Set in Palacio 10 on 11½ pt.
01 – 0988 – 58754

Typeset in Great Britain by JCL Graphics, Bristol

Made and printed in Great Britain

Because nothing could do that. Not now, not ever.

Ambermere was going to be hers one day, and she was going to care for it, and cherish it in a way her charming, happy-go-lucky father had never done. He called it openly the Albatross, and laughed at Julia's fury. Her month with Aunt Miriam had been a brief interval of rest and relaxation before she began the serious business of going into the Ambermere office with Mr Greenwood and learning how to run the estate. It was what she had always wanted, although Philip Kendrick had always insisted she would have changed her mind by the time she was old enough for such responsibility.

'We'll see how you feel when you're twenty-one,' he had told her briskly. And he'd been frankly astonished when her birthday had come and gone, and she was still of the same mind about what she wanted to do with her life.

And she would begin as she meant to go on by dealing with this tinker problem, swiftly and personally. If Loy thought she was going to be a pushover to deal with because she was a girl, he would soon discover his mistake!

She parked her car and walked through the copse. The shining trailers were parked neatly enough, but there seemed to be no one around except, for a tethered dog who barked aggressively at her as she passed.

She said, 'Shut up, Ben you idiot,' and knocked on the door of the largest and glossiest trailer.

It opened immediately, revealing a small, white-haired woman in a stridently floral overall. Blackberry-dark eyes surveyed the visitor gravely.

'Well, Miss Julia,' she said. 'It came to me that you'd be here today.'

Julia gave her a level look. Grandma Pascoe was reputed to have the second sight, and made a good income from telling fortunes at local fêtes and fairgrounds, but Julia had never believed the old woman had any special powers, just a good nose for gossip, and a phenomenal memory. And everyone in the county would know that no matter how long she'd been away, she would be back for tonight's party. No ESP required for that! she thought with a trace of cynicism.

She said, 'Hello, Grandma. Is Loy about?'

The white head moved in negation. 'He's seeing a man on business. Come in, Miss Julia. The kettle's boiled, and I've been spreading the cards for you.'

Julia hesitated. The tea would be welcome, but the last thing she wanted was Grandma brooding over the tarot cards on her behalf.

She began, 'I really don't think . . . ' but Grandma stopped her with an imperative gesture.

'You may not believe, missy, but there's a message for you just the same. I've been sitting waiting for you to come and hear it.'

And no doubt cross her palm with silver, the old crook, Julia thought, torn between amusement and annoyance, as she followed Grandma into the trailer and sat down opposite her at the table. The tea was scalding and almost black, and she sipped carefully, as Grandma began to turn over the cards in front of her.

''Tes all change for you, maiden, and a journey across water.'

'I've just done that,' Julia said wearily, Usually Grandma made at least a pretence of seeing the future.

'This is 'nother one.' Grandma gave her a gimlet look.

'I don't think so.' Julia shook her head. 'This time I'm here to stay.'

'See what covers you?' Grandma turned over another card, and gasped. 'The King of Swords! He's come to cut you off from all you know. He's terrible powerful, the King of Swords. You can't fight him, though you may try.'

'You can count on that,' Julia said drily. 'Can you tell me what he looks like, so I can be sure to avoid him?'

'He's close enough to touch.' Grandma's voice lowered to a whisper, and in spite of herself Julia felt a faint frisson of uneasiness chill her spine. 'And you can't avoid your fate, maiden.' She turned over the final card, and gasped again. 'See—the Tower struck by lightning. Your world turned upside down, and no mistake.'

Julia stared down at the card, her brows drawing together. She found herself wishing, ridiculously, that she'd bypassed the camp and let her father deal with the interloper. Then she pulled herself together. She had never been taken in by Grandma's nonsense before, and she certainly wasn't going to start now.

She drank the rest of her tea in one wincing gulp, and stood up. 'Well, the weather forecast says nothing about storms,' she remarked briskly. 'I'll take my chance.' She reached for her bag, but Grandma Pascoe shook her head.

'There's no need for money beween us, Miss Julia. I've given you the warning. I can do no more.' She paused. 'You're a proud girl, and no mistake, with a mind of your own. But that pride of yours will be brought low. It's all here.' She tapped the cards with a bony forefinger. 'Now run away home, and dance at your party while you can.'

Julia almost stumbled down the steps of the trailer, and paused, her heart thumping. There should be a law, she thought angrily, against Grandma Pascoe and her kind spreading forecasts of doom. It was all very different from the handsome husbands and football pools wins that the old lady generally predicted.

She sat in the car, letting her pulses slow to a more normal rate, castigating herself for being an idiot. And she hadn't even left a message for Loy about the trespasser, she realised vexedly, as she started her engine. Well, that would have to wait, because she certainly wasn't going back.

The yard at the back of the house which housed the former stables and the garages was crowded with vehicles, florists' and caterers' vans among them. There was the usual atmosphere of bustle and subdued panic that Julia always associated with the Midsummer party. Although heaven knows why, she told herself wryly, as she slid her car into its usual corner. Everything's always perfect, and this year even the weather's going to oblige us.

She found her mother in the large drawing-room, surrounded by lists. Lady Kendrick looked up as Julia walked towards her, her face breaking into a strained smile. 'Darling—at last!' She embraced her warmly.

'But you're very late. I was beginning to get anxious.'

'I took a slight detour,' Julia said with deliberate lightness. 'And I really wish I hadn't. She gave her mother a searching look. Had those worry lines round her mouth and eyes, the tension along her cheekbones, been there unnoticed before Julia went away? If so, perhaps these few weeks of separation had been a good thing if they'd taught her to be more perceptive. Lydia Kendrick had always been a highly strung, nervous woman, and the vagaries of life with her charming, feckless but much-loved husband had done little to ease the wear and tear on her nervous system.

'Is everything all right?' asked Julia anxiously.

'Everything's fine—and wonderful now that you're here. I can't wait to hear all the news about Miriam—and everyone. But there's so much to do.' Lydria Kendrick gestured helplessly about her, and Julia kissed her cheek.

'I'll go and unpack, then I'll pitch in and lend a hand with it all,' she promised reassuringly. 'Where's Daddy?'

'He's rather busy. Mr Poulton came down first thing this morning. They've been shut up in the study for most of the day.'

Julia's brows lifted. 'Rather inconsiderate of Polly,' she remarked, using her father's joking name for their staid family solicitor. 'He doesn't usually bother Daddy with business meetings on Midsummer Day.' She paused. 'Are you sure there's nothing wrong?'

'Of course not.' Her mother was smiling, but her glance slid away evasively. 'It's just—routine. Probably Polly underestimated the time it would take.'

There *is* something the matter, Julia thought as she unlocked her cases in her sunny bedroom and began to restore the contents to drawers and wardrobe. It wasn't just the uproar of preparing for the party either. It was like some dark and disturbing undercurrent beneath Ambermere's familiar and tranquil surface. From the moment she'd seen that man—that intruder in the lower paddock, her day had seemed disjointed, her homecoming oddly clouded.

'Jools, you're going crazy,' she adjured herself, as she unwrapped the dress she planned to wear that evening from its protective folds of tissue. Aunt Miriam had helped her choose it, and it relied for its chic on its stark and simple cut. She rarely wore that shade of midnight blue, but she had to admit Aunt Miriam was right when she said it darkened her eyes to sapphire. In the past, she'd chosen floating fabrics and pastels—débutante dresses, she thought with a slight grimace. This elegant, sophisticated model was going to open a few eyes—make it clear that Julia Kendrick was no longer a girl, but a woman ready and prepared to embark on her chosen course in life.

She sat down on her dressing stool and lifted her hair on top of her head in a casual swirl, studying herself, experimenting. The brief knock on her door made her start, and she looked up guiltily to see her mother had joined her.

'Are you waiting for me?' Julia jumped up. 'I'll only be a few minutes.'

'No—no. Everything's running like clockwork really—as it should after all these years.' Lydia Kendrick's voice was pitched higher than usual, and she dabbed at her mouth with a lace-edged handkerchief. 'Jools darling, I shouldn't be here talking to you like this. Your father told me to wait until after the party—not to spoil things for you on your first night—but I can't . . .'

Julia put a protective arm round the slender shoulders, helping her to the window seat and sitting beside her.

'What is it, love? Has Daddy been backing losers again? Is that why Polly's here, to give him the usual rap over the knuckles?'

Lydia gave a strangled sob. 'It's worse than that,' she said hoarsely. 'So much worse. I don't know how to tell you . . .' There was a pause while she obviously fought for control. Then she said brokenly, 'Jools—your father is having to sell this house.'

Julia had the oddest sensation that everything in the room had receded to a great distance. Her voice sounded very clear, however, and very cold.

'Is this some awful joke? Because I'm afraid I don't find it very funny . . .'

'Would I—could I joke about something like this?' Her mother's tone was piteous. 'Ambermere has to go. That's why Mr Poulton's here. He's been here every day almost for the past two weeks. Your—your father's had a lot of financial setbacks. The Mullion Corporation takeover—there was talk of insider trading—he had to resign from the board, although he swears he had nothing to do with it. And that's not all. Some time ago, Daddy changed a lot of our investments, because he felt we needed more return from our money. Some of the new investments were—high-risk, but he thought it was worth the gamble.' She swallowed nervously. 'We lost a great deal—too much. It's been a disaster. We have to sell Ambermere, Jools, because we can't afford to go on living here. The party tonight will be the last we'll ever give.' She began to cry, her throat wrenched by small gusty sobs.

Julia sat holding her, feeling frozen.

Worth the gamble, she thought. Those words had a hollow ring. All her life, her father had been a gambler, preferring to live his life on a knife-edge of insecurity. There were years when his betting and baccarat losses had been phenomenal. Julia could remember tearful scenes, and an atmosphere of gloomy repentance which she had only partly understood at the time.

Later, it had been explained to her that their income was adequate as long as they lived quietly and without undue extravagance. But that wasn't Philip Kendrick's way. Country life bored him, except in small doses. He was always looking out for some scheme which would restore the family fortunes to some fabled pre-war level. He'd been like some small boy, looking for adventure, she thought. But now the adventure had gone hideously wrong.

She said, 'Why—did Polly let him?'

'He didn't tell him anything about it until it was too late. You see, Daddy had been taking advice from some American he'd met in Monte Carlo—some financial wizard.' Lydia's lips tightened. 'Apparently this man's just been indicted for fraud in New York.'

Julia felt sick, 'Oh, God—Daddy's not involved in that?'

'Oh, no.' Lydia's fingers tore nervously at her

handkerchief, but her voice was decisively reassuring. 'Darling, I know how you must feel—but Daddy did this for the best. The costs of running a house like this, an estate like Ambermere, are punitively high. He wanted you to have—a proper inheritance, not to have to scrimp and save all your life.'

Julia felt immensely weary. 'Why didn't you tell me—call me back from Aunt Miriam's?'

'We wanted you to have a good time. And there was nothing you could have done.'

'There must be something. I'm not going to let Ambermere go like this.' Julia tried to smile. 'Perhaps no one will want to buy the Albatross. No one we know has that kind of money.'

There was a long silence, then Lydia said quietly, 'These days, darling, estates like this tend to look for buyers from abroad. And Mr Poulton has found one for us.'

'Abroad?' Julia echoed dazedly. She shook her head. 'Not some Arab prince? I don't believe it . . .'

'Not quite. In fact——' there were bright spots of colour burning in her mother's cheeks '—I would almost prefer it. This man is Greek—a so-called tycoon. His name is Alexandros Constantis.'

'Constantis?' Julia's brows snapped together. 'That's familiar. Does he have a relative called Paul?'

'I wouldn't know,' Lady Kendrick said with distaste. 'What I've heard of his antecedents is bad enough. I have no wish to enquire into his immediate family. Not that they have very much to do with him,' she added with unaccustomed waspishness.

'Then it must be the same man,' Julia said slowly,

thinking, remembering. 'I had dinner with Paul Constantis a few times—he was charming. He had a post at the Greek Embassy—something fairly junior, I gathered, but he used to joke about nature having intended him to be a millionaire until fate, in the shape of his cousin Alex, had prevented it.'

'Poor boy,' Lydia Kendrick said, almost fiercely. 'I imagine that's only too true. You're too young to remember the scandal, of course, but George Constantis was an immensely wealthy man, with a fortune in banking and property all over the Mediterranean. He was a widower, and childless, and his estate was expected to go to his sister and her children. Then lo and behold, on his deathbed, he suddenly revealed that he had an illegitimate son and had left his entire business empire to this child.' She shook her head. 'The family wouldn't have objected to some kind of provision, naturally, but to have this person no one had ever known existed foisted on to them—over them—was appalling. He wasn't a child, of course. He was already a grown man—but it was said he'd been dragged up in total poverty in some slum, and could barely read or write. There was some mystery about the mother, apparently. It seems she was some little peasant girl Constantis had seduced.

'They fought, of course. They tried to prove he wasn't Constantis's son at all, insisted on blood tests, but they were inconclusive, so then they tried to overturn the will in the courts, saying this Alex had exerted undue influence on the old man while he was ill. It was quite a *cause célèbre*. But they lost—and he took everything.'

And now, Julia thought, rage rising inside her, now

he's trying to take Ambermere from me. But he won't. Not someone like that.

'An uncouth barbarian,' Paul Constantis had called him, she remembered. Well he wasn't going to lay his vandal's hands on her home, if she could prevent it!

She got to her feet, 'I'm going down to talk to Daddy,' she said, trying to keep her voice level. 'There must be something we can do. And surely this Constantis creature can't be the only prospective buyer we can find?'

'Apparently he's made an excellent offer,' her mother returned. 'He does a great deal of business over here, and wants a permanent residence where he can entertain.'

'Bouzouki nights with plate smashing, no doubt,' Julia said grimly, moving to the door. 'We'll see about that!' She ran along the gallery and down the wide curve of the big staircase, letting her hand slide down the highly polished balustrade as she had always done. As she always would do, she told herself. Ambermere had to be saved somehow.

As she reached the foot of the stairs, the study door opened and her father emerged with Gordon Poulton at his side. He looked tired and haggard, and in spite of her bitterness Julia felt a wrench of her heart at his obvious distress.

He looked up and saw her, and tried to smile. 'Jools, sweetheart, no one told me you were home. 'How marvellous!'

She ran to him. 'Daddy, tell me it's not true. Promise me you haven't sold Ambermere to this appalling Greek peasant!'

She heard Gordon Poulton make a shocked noise, and saw her father's brows snap together in sudden quelling anger. From the shadowy doorway behind them, a third figure detached itself and stepped forward.

Julia felt as if a hand had closed round her throat. She knew him at once, of course. It was the man she'd seen in the lower paddock and taken for a tinker.

No wonder he'd laughed at her! she thought dazedly.

Only this time he wasn't laughing at all. As the hooded dark gaze swept her from head to foot, she felt as if the flesh had been scorched from her bones by some swift and terrifying flame.

It was all she could do not to fling up her hands to defend herself.

The Tower struck by lightning, she thought, from some whirling corner of her mind, and the King of Swords, coming to cut down her pride and separate her from everything she loved.

CHAPTER TWO

THE SAPPHIRE dress looked superb. Julia regarded herself critically in the full-length mirror, making a minute adjustment to the seams of her stockings, and tucking an errant strand of hair into place in her carefully casual topknot.

She looked elegant, poised and sophisticated—just as the daughter of the house should, she thought bitterly. But she was only attending the party under protest, and after the most thunderous row she'd ever had with her father. Even the thought of it now could still make her shudder.

'How dare you, Julia!' Sir Philip's voice had been glacial, when they were finally alone together. 'I'd hoped your time with Miriam might have cured you of your tendency to impulsive and inopportune reactions. You realise nothing is signed yet between Constantis and myself, and you could have jeopardised the negotiations by your insolence?'

'Then I'm glad,' she had answered defiantly. 'Daddy, you can't sell Ambermere to a man like that! There must be some other way.'

'If there was, then I'd have found it.' His tone sharpened. 'You're a child, Julia—a spoiled child. I've done you no favours by sheltering you from life's realities.'

'Is that how you categorise Alex Constantis?'

Julia's laugh broke in the middle. 'Then I'm glad you did—shelter me. He can't have Ambermere—he can't!'

'He can—and I desperately hope he will.' She had never seen her father look so stern. 'And you, madam, will do and say nothing else to put the sale at risk.'

'Well, you have no need to worry about that.' Julia glared back at him. 'I'll make very sure our paths don't cross again!'

'In fact you'll meet him again this evening,' Sir Philip told her grimly. 'He's dining with us, and staying on for the party.'

Julia's lips parted in a despairing gasp. 'You can't have invited him!' she wailed. 'Not someone like that. Our friends will think we approve of him—that we're endorsing him in some way.'

'And why shouldn't we?' Sir Philip slammed his desk with a clenched fist. 'My God, Julia. Where did you learn to be such an appalling little snob? Alex Constantis may have inherited money initially, but he's made another fortune on his own account since he became head of the Constantis empire. And in today's world, it's money that counts, my dear, as I'm afraid you're going to find out. So far, he's been reasonably accommodating. I just pray you haven't ruined everything with your muddle-headed stupidity. He has a reputation for being a tough operator.'

'For being a bastard!' Julia flung back at him. 'Which is, of course, exactly what he is.'

'And what have we, precisely, to be so stately and moral about?' Sir Philip demanded. 'If the first Julia Kendrick hadn't caught the Prince Regent's eye, then we would never have owned Ambermere in the first place. Perhaps you should remember that.' He paused, surveying her defiant, tight-lipped face. 'And remember this too, Jools. Tonight I expect you to be civil to Alex Constantis—beginning, perhaps, with an apology.'

'Will a plain "sorry I spoke" do, or would you like me to grovel—lick his shoes even?'

And so it had gone on, covering the same wretched ground, the same recriminations, until finally they had reached a kind of armed truce. Julia did not have to apologise in so many words, but she wouldn't be allowed to feign a headache and miss the party either. And she would be polite to Alex Constantis.

'I know it's a terrible situation for you, darling,' her father had said more gently, just before she went up, reluctantly, to change. 'But we're still a family, and that's what matters in the end. Bricks and mortar, however historic, aren't that important.'

The trouble was, Julia thought dispiritedly, her father had right on his side. She had been abysmally rude about Alex Constantis. But how could she have known he was lurking about in the study doorway like the Demon King, ready to pop up at just the wrong moment? And if she had known would she honestly have behaved differently? Somehow, she doubted it.

And where rudeness was concerned, honours were about even, she thought. He had snubbed her totally and succinctly, after her father had awkwardly attempted to introduce them, reminding Sir Philip coolly that they were due to visit the Home Farm, and walking off with him without deigning Julia a second look.

But that was all to the good, Julia thought, her mouth suddenly dry. Because if the second look lived up to the first, she might end up permanently singed.

There was little doubt that the evening ahead was going to be an ordeal. Her father had made it clear that he intended to introduce Alex Constantis to their neighbours and friends as the future owner of Ambermere, and Julia wasn't at all sure she could bear it.

She had almost decided against wearing the new dress, telling herself that it didn't matter what she looked like—that the oldest rag in the wardrobe would do for a—awake like this evening promised to be.

But her pride had reasserted itself. Her ship might be sinking, but she would nail her full colours to the mast—and she would let no one, but no one know how much she despised and resented Alex Constantis. Her innate realism told her that too many avid eyes would be watching for any sign of grief or distress. Their friends would understand and sympathise, she thought with a sigh, but there were others in the neighbourhood, less well disposed towards the Kendricks, who had been prophesying doom and disaster for years.

And now the doom had come upon them in the unwelcome shape of this—Greek upstart, she thought wretchedly.

Paul Constantis had been philosophical about the enforced change in his circumstances, but Julia had sensed an underlying bitterness. She'd sympathised with him, without feeling too involved, but she was concerned now all right. Because by some incredible, nauseating coincidence, Alex Constantis was going to take Ambermere from her, just as he'd preyed on the Constantis family fortune. He was going to steal her home.

'Bricks and mortar aren't important,' Sir Philip had said.

Not to you, Daddy, Julia thought in aching silence. Never to you—but to me.

She was aware that her love for Ambermere was a local byword, could imagine the shock waves when people realised this would be the last Midsummer party. But no one would pity her tonight—or laugh at her either, she told herself almost savagely, as she lifted her scent spray and misted herself with fragrance before turning resolutely to the door and making her way downstairs.

It was still quite early, and the special guests who had been invited to dinner before the party proper began had not begun to arrive yet, so Julia expected to have the drawing-room to herself for a while.

But to her horror, Alex Constantis was there before her, standing on the hearthrug, staring up at the enormous portrait of the Regency Julia Kendrick which hung above the fireplace. Twentieth-century Julia had never cared for this constant reminder of how her family had acquired Ambermere. She had always been vaguely embarrassed by the pride of place given to a woman who had shamelessly betrayed her husband, and behaved like a tart with Prinny. And she loathed the lighthearted family tradition of drinking a toast to the first Julia as a climax to the Midsummer party. But perhaps, in the circumstances, that particular ritual could be forgone this year.

She hesitated in the doorway, wondering whether she could steal away before he saw her, but the wretched man must have had eyes in the back of his head, because without turning, he said, 'Come in, *thespinis*, and tell me about your ancestress.'

Julia came forward with deep unwillingness, strongly tempted to repudiate all knowledge of the flame-haired beauty in her shockingly fashionable transparent draperies.

But before she could speak, he added drily, 'And do not try to deny the relationship. The family resemblance is there—and the colour of the hair.' He turned and looked at her fully, the glittering dark gaze sliding with unabashed interest over the untrammelled cling of the midnight dress. 'And the fact that you both wear so little,' he ended silkily.

In spite of herself, Julia felt dull colour rise in her face. The cut of the dress demanded a minimum of underwear, but it infuriated her that this stranger—this interloper, should be so immediately aware of the fact—and be graceless enough to refer to it.

At the same time she was forced to acknowledge that his voice was attractive—low-pitched and resonant, with barely a trace of an accent. Not, she thought, what she would have expected from someone of his background.

She said coolly, 'As you're a stranger to Britain, Mr Constantis, perhaps I should warn you that sexist remarks are no longer welcomed here.'

'Sexist?' Alex Constantis repeated the word as if it were utterly new to him, then shrugged. 'Yet we are still born male and female, *thespinis*. The human race does not yet allow for neuters. Nor will it continue for much longer unless a man is able to tell a woman that he finds her desirable.'

To her fury, Julia felt her flush deepen. Did this person actually mean . . . No, of course he didn't. He was simply getting his own back by deliberately setting out to embarrass her.

She said crisply, 'You were asking about the portrait, I believe. She was the wife of the first baronet, and her name was Julia.'

'You were named for her?'

'Yes.' Julia forbore to add 'unfortunately', knowing it would involve her in explanations which she didn't wish to give. Alex Constantis's grin was far too insolent already.

He glanced back at the portrait. 'She is very beautiful. To possess such loveliness would be a rare acquisition.'

Again Julia had the uneasy feeling that his remark was a loaded one, intended to needle her. At this rate, she thought crossly, I'll be spending the entire evening blushing like a schoolgirl!

She forced her voice to remain level. 'I'm afraid the portrait isn't for sale, Mr Constantis. You're buying a house, not a family history.'

He said softly, 'The past does not concern me, *thespinis*—only the present—and the future. And it is not altogether certain that I shall buy Ambermere.'

Julia groaned inwardly. Aloud, she said stiffly, 'If you're having second thoughts because of anything I've said or done, then I'm sorry.'

'Are you?' He spoke in the same reflective tone, but

Julia felt an inexplicable shiver run down her spine—as if he'd threatened her in some way.

Oh, I'm being ridiculous, she thought with exasperation.

She tried to speak lightly. 'Perhaps we'd better declare a truce. May I offer you a drink?'

'Thank you. Do you have Bourbon?'

'Of course. It's what my father drinks.' Julia moved to the side table where the decanters stood, and poured a measure into a glass, angrily aware that her hands were shaking.

'Come on, Jools,' she whispered to herself. 'Get it together.'

To add to her self-consciousness, she felt certain Alex Constantis had spotted her nervousness, and was amused by it, although his expression when she handed him the glass was enigmatic.

'You are not joining me?' he asked, and Julia shook her head.

'It's going to be a long evening,' she excused herself, with a bright smile which only touched her lips.

'Then—yiassou.' He raised his glass to her, then drank.

Julia began to wish she had in fact poured herself a drink as well. It would have given her something to fidget with—to concentrate on—anything rather than just having to stand here, the object of his undivided attention.

'So, tell me more about your namesake,' he said, after a pause. 'She was the mistress of the Prince of Wales—isn't that right?'

Julia's lips tightened. 'You seem perfectly well

informed already.'

'There is a small bookshop opposite my hotel in the village. I bought a local guide book, and such a story was mentioned.'

She shrugged. 'Then what more is there to tell?'

'Her husband—this first baronet. What kind of a man was he?'

'He was one of the Prince's circle,' Julia said reluctantly. 'Though not a close friend. He was a gambler.'

'So that is where the tendency comes from,' Alex Constantis said meditatively. 'Was he also as unlucky as your father?'

Julia shot him a look of indignant surprise, annoyed at the implied criticism in his words. 'I don't think I want to discuss that with you.'

'Yet it has a certain relevance.' The dark eyes were hooded. 'If your father had been luckier in his wagers—in his speculation, then your family home would not be for sale to the highest bidder—and we would not be here together now.'

She said tautly, 'Please don't remind me.'

He laughed. 'The truce did not last long, *thespinis*. But no matter. My instinct tells me that to war with you might be more interesting than to make peace.'

'And your instinct, of course, is never wrong.' Julia was heavily sarcastic.

'Where women are concerned—rarely.' He was still smiling. 'Another sexist remark!'

Julia bit her lip. 'Could we change the subject, please?'

'Certainly.' He drank some more Bourbon. 'Shall we talk about the weather, or shall I tell you how beautiful you look in that dress, and how much I would give to see you without it?'

Shame and anger welled up inside her, as if she had indeed been stripped naked in front of him. If she had had a drink in her hand, she would have thrown it straight into his mocking, arrogant face, she thought savagely. She wanted to hit out, to beat at him with her fists, but she knew, somehow, that such a gesture would only amuse him.

My God, she thought. He's demanding a full pound of flesh in return for my having called him a peasant!

From somewhere she managed to conjure up a light laugh. 'Would you give me Ambermere, Mr Constantis?'

His brows lifted slightly, as if her reaction had surprised him, and he said, 'No.'

Julia shrugged again. 'Then the deal's off.' She made herself meet his gaze. 'You'll just have to—eat your heart out.'

His smile widened, and he shook his head slowly. 'Don't count on it—Miss Kendrick.'

For an endless moment his eyes held hers. Julia was suddenly, terrifyingly conscious that she could neither move nor speak—and that every pulse point in her body seemed to be beating with an alarming independence.

She wanted to say 'No.' To assert her separateness from him, her rejection of him, and his degrading jibes, but the muscles of her throat refused to obey her.

It was the external sound of other voices, and footsteps approaching down the hall, which broke the spell at last. And if she'd burned before, Julia now realised she felt icily, deathly cold.

As Alex Constantis turned to greet her parents, she crossed to the empty fireplace and stood staring down at it, as if there were flames there which could warm her, and stop the wild, inner shivering which threatened to tear her apart.

Lydia Kendrick was polite to her unwanted guest, but there was none of her usual warmth in her manner, and Julia surmised that she too was under orders.

Her father seemed his usual ebullient self, laughing and talking as if Alex Constantis was an old and valued friend, but Julia could see the lines of strain round his mouth, and thought how they would deepen if the offer for the house was withdrawn.

She felt as if she was living through some kind of nightmare.

She had hoped the situation would be eased when the other dinner guests arrived, but among the first-comers were the Bosworths, and Vivvy Bosworth lost no time in drawing Julia into the morning-room.

'Jools, there are the most amazing rumours all over the place. People are saying your father's sold the estate to some Greek millionaire. Surely it can't be true?'

Julia pinned on a smile. 'We're certainly hoping the deal goes through.'

'Oh, don't con me, Julia Kendrick!' Vivvy gave her a minatory look. 'I've known you far too long—we swapped rattles in our prams, remember? You'd rather lose your right arm than this house.'

Julia's smile wavered and collapsed. She said

wretchedly, 'Oh Vivvy, the house is going to be sold whatever happens, but I honestly don't know whether Alex Constantis is going to buy Ambermere or not.' She swallowed. 'What I do know is I'd sooner see it burn to the ground than belong to him. He's the most hateful man I've ever met!'

Vivvy gave her a limpid look. 'Darling Jools, no man with all that money could possibly be hateful!' She sobered, giving Julia a quick hug. 'There's nothing I can say to make you feel better about this, but I felt I had to warn you. Stepmother's on the warpath. She was smirking to herself all the way here, and that's always bad news for someone.'

Julia received the news with a grimace of dismay. Gerald Bosworth's first wife had been a warm and smiling woman, popular with everyone, and genuinely mourned when she died after a long illness. It was generally agreed locally that Gerald, who had nursed her with total devotion, should marry again in due time, but no one, least of all Vivvy and her brother Alastair, had expected it to happen so soon, or to find themselves with a young and glamorous former actress as a stepmother. Tricia Bosworth at first bewildered her new neighbours, who tried to make her welcome for Gerald's sake, and later aroused their resentment with the deliberately poisonous sweetness of some of her remarks. Because she was Gerald's wife, and everyone liked Gerald, it was impossible to exclude her from social gatherings, but there was always an edge when she was around.

'An actress!' Julia had once said bitterly, smarting from Tricia's smiling comments about adolescent gaucherie. 'What's she ever been in, for heaven's sake?'

'She claims to have been in an RSC production of *Antony and Cleopatra,*' Vivvy had returned dejectedly. 'Probably playing the asp.'

Tricia had always gushed about Ambermere, its beauty and its history, but she wouldn't be shedding any tears over the Kendricks' loss, and the thought of her openly probing their wounds over dinner was unbearable.

What else can go wrong? Julia asked herself unhappily. How could the passage of a few hours change one's entire life so fundamentally?

'Cheer up.' Vivvy linked an arm through hers. 'She may choke on a fishbone and die before she can start.'

Julia smiled reluctantly. 'Can't we arrange for two fishbones?'

'Never kill off a millionaire unless you're mentioned in his will,' Vivvy warned solemnly. 'What's he like—old, fat and repulsive?'

'No,' Julia said colourlessly. 'I suppose he's attractive—if you like that sort of thing.'

'I'm sure I could learn to,' giggled Vivvy. 'Lead me to him!'

As Julia took her into the drawing-room, she gave vent to a soundless whistle. 'Attractive? My God, Jools, are you crazy? He's gorgeous!'

Unwillingly, Julia had to concede that Vivvy spoke with a certain justice. In the casual clothes he had been wearing when she first encountered him, he'd looked a force to be reckoned with. Now, in the dark formality of dinner jacket and black tie, Alex

Constantis possessed a disturbing, charismatic presence which was drawing every female eye in the room.

Well, they said wealth and power were aphrodisiacs, Julia thought savagely, then bit her lip. She was being unfair, and she knew it. Even if he were penniless, any woman with blood in her veins would look at him, and look again. Except me, she reminded herself grimly.

But that was not as easy as it seemed. To her chagrin, Julia found she was placed opposite him at the long oak table in the dining-room, and no matter how rigorously she limited her attention to the companions on either side of her, she was still uneasily aware that he was watching her across the heaped bowls of early roses, and the flickering candle flames.

Tricia Bosworth leaned forward. 'So you're going to be the new master of Ambermere,' she said in her husky drawl. 'Do tell us—has Julia persuaded you to change your name to Kendrick yet?'

Julia put her knife and fork down, her mouth suddenly dry.

Alex Constantis's brows lifted. 'I do not quite understand.'

Mrs Bosworth laughed. 'Oh, it's been a standing joke locally for years. Julia has always sworn that the family name should continue here—either by finding another Kendrick from somewhere to marry her, or forcing some other unsuspecting soul to change his name. I wondered if she'd started her campaign with you yet. She's always claimed to be prepared to go to any lengths to keep Ambermere hers.'

'So I have already gathered.' The faint irony in his voice, and the flickering glance he sent the deeply slashed bodice of the midnight blue satin dress, were not lost on Julia.

'I'm sure you have,' purred Tricia then she paused, smiling. 'Are you married, Mr Constantis?'

The dark face was shuttered. 'No.'

In the hideously embarrassed silence which followed, Julia prayed for the floor beneath her chair to open, and swallow her for ever. She heard Gerald Bosworth mutter, 'Tricia, for God's sake!' and saw Vivvy's appalled and sympathetic grimace.

Into the silence, Sir Philip said pleasantly, 'As you say, Mrs Bosworth—a standing joke. But I don't think Julia, as a woman, should have a silly childhood boast held against her. Now, may I offer you some more duck?'

Conversation around the table resumed again in an atmosphere of relief, which Julia could not share. If Tricia Bosworth had openly gloated that Ambermere had to be sold, it would have been bad enough, but the other woman had deliberately set out to humiliate her in front of Alex Constantis. If she'd received a blow-by-blow account of the day's events she couldn't have planted her barbs more effectively, Julia thought, wincing.

And only he would not be aware that Tricia Bosworth made a speciality of such malice.

And somehow she had to smile and go on, pretending it didn't matter. She took a surreptitious glance at her small gold watch, wondering how long it would be before she could make some excuse and seek the refuge of her room.

Tonight, as never before, she found herself welcoming the duties as hostess with her mother which kept her perpetually on the move from group to group as the house filled with guests.

She had half expected, half dreaded that Alex Constantis would seek her out with some taunting reference to Tricia's words. But perhaps he too had been embarrassed by the exchange, for he never came near her.

Her father was almost always at his side, guiding him through the crowded rooms explaining, making introductions, while their friends loyally strove to mask their surprise and dismay at the news.

And even now it could all be for nothing, Julia thought with misgivings. Wouldn't it be hysterical if Tricia proves to be the final straw, and the whole deal falls through? But she didn't feel much like laughing. Even if Alex Constantis withdrew from contention, another buyer would come along. Ambermere could not be saved, and she had to come to terms with that.

As midnight approached Julia realised that the toast to the first Lady Kendrick was going to be drunk as usual.

'Oh, God, I can't face that,' she muttered to herself, slipping through the partially open french windows on to the terrace.

There was no breeze, but the night air felt refreshingly cool against her uncovered shoulders and arms. A scent of flowers hung in the air, making her starkly, poignantly aware that this was the last Midsummer night she would ever spend in this house.

She leaned on the balustrade, gazing sightlessly

over the starlit gardens, wondering painfully what changes Alex Constantis would make if he bought the house. He would probably plough up the south lawn and replace it with a swimming pool, and a helicopter pad, she thought scornfully, and she should be glad she wasn't going to be around to see such desecration.

She could hear the laughter and the cheering from the drawing room, and the cries of 'To Julia', which followed her father's traditional, humorous speech, and wondered how many of the particpants realised they were drinking the toast for the last time. Julia Kendrick—scandalous wife, daring mistress, Toast of the Town—had reached the end of her reign.

She felt sudden absurd tears sting at her eyelids, and thought, 'To Julia'. And heard, with sudden shock, the same words echoed aloud from only a feet away.

She whirled round, her hands flying to her mouth to cover the little startled cry forced from her. 'You!'

'Yes,'

Somehow, in the shadows of the night, he looked taller—more powerful than ever, the dark face an unreadable mask as he stood between her and the sanctuary of the lighted window.

He said, 'I came to wish you goodnight, *thespinis.*'

'You're—leaving?' The words seemed to twist out of her suddenly dry throat.

He smiled. 'That is what you're hoping for, *ne?*' He shook his head. 'I am sorry to disappoint you. I shall be back—later today.'

'You're going to buy the house?'

'I think so. You have rekindled my interest in it.'

'I—have?'

'Certainly. Ambermere must be a unique property, if it can rouse such passionate commitment in you.' He paused. 'I wonder, in different circumstances, if you would ever have found the husband you are looking for, Julia Kendrick—a man so little a man he would deny his name and his birthright in subjection to your whim.'

'It wasn't a whim,' she denied huskily. 'How could you possibly understand?'

'You think perhaps that I have no right to the name I bear?' The dark eyes glittered at her. 'Well, you are not the first to say so—even though there have been few who would dare utter the words to my face.'

'Because they're all so terrified of you?' Her voice sounded high and rather breathless. 'When you take Ambermere, you'll have done the worst you can. You have no power over me after that.'

'You don't think so?' Slowly he advanced on her, making her retreat until her back was pressed against the balustrade with no further physical withdrawal possible. 'But you are wrong, Julia Kendrick. Because if I take Ambermere, I shall also take you.'

His hands descended on her shoulders. He used no particular force, but with the first shock of his touch on her bare skin, Julia knew her flesh would bear the imprint of his fingers as if he had bruised her.

She tried to say 'No!' but he was bending towards her, shutting out safety, blocking the starlight, and the word was stifled on her lips by the stark, demanding pressure of his mouth. She tried to resist, to keep her own mouth closed against his insistence, but it was a battle she could not win. A battle he was determined, with total sensuality, that she should lose.

In some distant corner of her mind, she admitted this. Recognised that this confrontation had been inevitable since she had entered the drawing-room that night.

A sigh trembled through her, and she capitulated, allowing him to invade her mouth and deepen the kiss in any way he wanted. But even that was not enough. His lips, his tongue demanded a response she had never before been required to give—a response she wasn't even sure she capable of. She couldn't breathe, and her legs seemed to be turning to water, as his hands pushed the straps of her dress from her shoulders, then drew her against him so that her bared breasts were brought into aching, erotic contract with the hard wall of his chest.

And from somewhere in her innermost being, she felt the first slow uncurling of heated, treacherous, unbearable excitement.

Her hands went up to clasp the lapels of his jacket as an insidious weakness began to spread through her. When he took his mouth from hers, she gasped, her head falling back helplessly as his mouth traced a path down the column of her throat.

But as his hand lifted to close intimately on one small naked breast, she cried out in outraged modesty, summoning all the strength of will which still remained to her in order to drag herself out of his arms. She was shaking so much she thought she might fall, her hands fumbling as she tried to drag her dress back into place, to hide her body from that dark, devouring gaze.

For one shuddering moment she thought he might reach for her again, and shrank back against the support of the balustrade.

She heard him catch his breath, and saw the savage, single-minded hunger die from his face, to be replaced by an odd wryness.

He said, to himself, 'A virgin. And that, of course, changes everything.'

Then, before Julia could move or speak, he turned, and walked away from her into the darkness.

CHAPTER THREE

JULIA stayed in her room until late the following morning. Downstairs she could hear the whine of vacuum cleaners, and a subdued hum of voices and movement, as the small army of cleaners from the village restored order after the party. Normally, she would have got up and pitched in with them.

But this time she didn't seem capable of doing anything but lying staring at the ceiling, letting the events of the previous day, and more particularly, the previous night, re-run in her mind like some slow-moving action replay.

It was still impossible for her to believe that she had behaved like that—responded like that, especially with a man she resented and despised. She even wondered whether she had dreamed the whole thing.

It had been, after all, Midsummer Night. But Alex Constantis's kisses were far from being 'the stuff that dreams are made on', Julia thought wryly.

And she couldn't blame alcohol either, for she'd hardly drunk anything all night.

Oh, damn him, she thought savagely, burying her face in the pillow. Damn him to hell!

Her behaviour had been totally out of context with the rest of her life. She had never been the type to walk willingly into any man's arms. 'Passionately

41

aloof' had been the rueful description from one of her
admirers, and she had liked that. She'd had a life
planned out for herself in security and harmony at
Ambermere, and nothing was going to interfere with
that, especially the kind of casual sexual diversion so
many of her friends seemed to take for granted. True,
the threat of serious disease had changed their
thinking in recent months, but Julia had had to make
no such adaptation.

I was fashionable without even knowing it, she told
herself half derisively.

Now she was being forced to consider whether the
strong-mindedness she had always prided herself on
might not simply have been lack of serious
temptation.

No, she thought, thumping the mattress with her
fist. I won't believe that. Yesterday I was knocked
sideways by the news about Ambermere, that's all,
and I went a little mad. But today I'm sane again.

Sane enough, certainly, to think about plans for her
drastically altered future.

Soberly, she considered her strengths in book-
keeping and word-processing which she had
intended to use in the administration of the estate,
working alongside her father. Surely they were
sufficient to find her some kind of secretarial work.
And a number of her former school friends were now
living and working in London, and always looking
for an extra flatmate to help out with the rent.

I'll survive, she told herself. I'll have to.

She got up, took a quick bath, then dressed in jeans
and a shirt before going downstairs.

Mrs Parsons the housekeeper was coming along

the hall with a tray of coffee for Sir Philip's study, and Julia followed her.

'Morning, Jools.' Her father's greeting was a shade over-hearty. 'You slipped away rather early last night, didn't you?'

'I wasn't really in a party mood,' Julia returned levelly, and Sir Philip nodded, shuffling the papers on his desk.

'It's a hell of a thing,' he said sombrely. 'Jools, if there was any other way, you know—don't you . . .'

'Yes,' Julia acknowledged with a sigh, 'I know.' She poured out the coffee and handed her father his cup. 'Although I suppose nothing's settled yet.'

'As a matter of fact it is.' Her father gave her an awkward glance. 'Alex Constantis telephoned after breakfast to confirm his offer. Polly and I are meeting his lawyers this afternoon to work out the final details. It's all going to happen rather fast, I suspect.'

'I'm sure it will,' Julia agreed drily. Even when he was standing still, Alex Constantis gave an impression of being consumed by restless dynamic energy. Once he had made up his mind he wanted something, he would allow no grass to grow under his feet until he possessed it, she thought, a frisson of unease prickling between her shoulderblades.

'He's coming over later,' her father went on. 'We spent rather a long time at the Home Farm yesterday, and he wants to see the rest of the estate.' He paused. 'I told him you'd be happy to be his guide.'

'You said what?' Julia sent him a horrified glance. 'Oh, Daddy, you couldn't have done! I never want to set eyes on that man again as long as I live!'

'Then that's unfortunate.' Sir Philip frowned.

'What I said yesterday, Jools, still applies. I expect you to be civil, and keep any personal antipathy you may feel under control. Nothing's actually signed yet, after all. And you're the best person anyway for a job like that. Constantis was asking me last night about the damnfool remarks that silly woman poor Gerald lumbered himself with was making at dinner, and I explained to him how much the estate meant to you. He was very understanding.'

'I'm sure he was,' Julia said bitterly. She sighed. 'All right then, Daddy, I'll do what you want, on condition it's the last time I have to meet Mr Constantis. Tomorrow I'm going to London to start job-hunting.'

Sir Philip stared at her. 'But there's no need for that. Once the estate is sold, we won't be penniless. I thought we might move to the Riviera, or somewhere in the sun. These English winters are no good for Mummy's chest, you know, and . . .'

'No darling,' Julia said gently. 'You two go ahead and make whatever plans you want. I have to start organising a life for myself.' She lifted her chin. 'I'm not a child any more.'

'No,' Sir Philip said rather sadly, 'I suppose not.'

An hour later Julia waved her parents a smiling goodbye. Lydia Kendrick had decided to accompany her husband to London to do some shopping, a decision which Julia suspected sprang from the news that Alex Constantis was due at Ambermere shortly.

Lucky Mother, she thought with a sigh. I wish I could cut and run!

As she went back into the house, the telephone rang, and she reached for it with a feeling of foreboding. But it was only Vivvy.

'Where did you disappear to last night?' her friend asked plaintively.

'I began to feel like the skeleton at the feast and went to bed,' Julia excused herself.

'Not swept off your feet by the dishy Mr Constantis, I hope,' giggled Vivvy, then she lowered her voice conspiratorially. 'By the way, Jools, Dad and Stepmother had a mega-row last night over her remarks at dinner. Alastair and I could hear them in their bedroom shouting at each other. I think Dad's rose-coloured glasses have cracked at last.'

'I'm sorry,' said Julia, and meant it.

'I'm not,' Vivvy returned with equal sincerity. 'She's an utter bitch, and everyone could see it but him. But she'll have to be more careful in future, which can only be a step in the right direction.' She paused. 'Actually, I thought Alex Constantis handled the situation pretty well. He's incredibly glamorous and sexy, Jools. Pity he's not looking for a wife, really.'

'Well, he'll be here at any minute for a tour of the estate,' Julia said coolly. 'I'll put in a good word for you.'

'For me?' Vivvy shrieked. 'Don't be an idiot! I was thinking of you. Tricia may have been out to make trouble, but she had a point, actually. If you married Alex Constantis, you'd still have Ambermere.'

'Thank you,' Julia said drily. 'But there's a limit to the sacrifices I'm prepared to make, even for Ambermere.'

Vivvy giggled again. 'Some sacrifice,' she said caustically. 'Quite apart from his money, I bet he's fantastic in bed.'

For one frightened moment Julia found herself re-
living the reality of being in Alex Constantis's arms.
The remembered scent of his skin, the warmth of his
body seemed to fill her senses, as if he had been
standing there beside her. A shiver ran through her.
She gave a shaky laugh.

'You're the limit. Viv! What would Reverend
Mother say if she could hear you?'

'She'd sigh, and offer to pray for me again,' Vivvy
said ebulliently. 'Poor soul, I bet she's never off her
knees.'

Julia's hand was trembling as she replaced the
receiver on the rest after Vivvy had rung off. Her
friend had only been joking, she knew, but her starlit
encounter with Alex Constantis had taught her
swiftly that any involvement with him was no
laughing matter.

'If I take Ambermere, I shall also take you.' The
words seemed to sting in her brain.

The only reassurance she could draw from the
incident was the change of heart he'd undergone
once he'd concluded she was a virgin. Although
heaven alone knew how he'd guessed that, she
thought with embarrassment. But clearly her total
lack of sexual experience was a drawback as far as he
was concerned.

And a lifesaver to me, she thought, squaring her
shoulders, as she heard the sound of a car on the
drive outside. She wiped suddenly damp hands on
her denim-clad thighs. And now it was daylight, and
the sexy party gear was shut away, along with the
madness which had afflicted her last night. She was

her practical workaday self once again.

There's nothing to fear, she told herself. Nothing.

She went out of the front door and stood looking down at him as he got out of the car. A new Aston Martin, she noticed in passing.

Alex Constantis walked to the foot of the steps and paused, a faint smile playing round his mouth as he surveyed her.

'*Kalimera*,' he said softly. 'Did you sleep well?'

I won't blush, Julia vowed silently and grimly. I bloody well won't!

She said coolly and untruthfully, 'Perfectly, thank you.'

'You are fortunate, Julia *mou*. Each time I closed my eyes, I dreamed you were beside me, and reached for you.' His smile widened. 'It was frustrating, believe me!'

Thrust deep into the pockets of her jeans, Julia's hands clenched into tense fists, then relaxed.

She said crisply. 'You may find such remarks amusing, Mr Constantis. I find them embarrassing and degrading.'

'Do you always find the truth disturbing? Or am I the first man brave enough to admit that he wants you in his bed?'

'Well, I don't want you,' Julia said sharply, aware of the deep, uneven throb of her pulses. 'I think you'd better go.'

'When I've seen the rest of the estate. Your father assured me you'd be delighted to be my guide.'

'That's his first mistake today. As he has to deal with your lawyers, I hope it's the last.' She glanced at her watch. 'Perhaps we could make it a quick tour.

I'm afraid I can't offer you lunch . . .'

'I do not expect you to,' he said silkily. 'I have brought a picnic for us to share. And the tour will take as long as necessary. You are, after all, the expert.' He paused. 'And I do not want statistics about yield per acre, either, *thespinis*. I want to see this land, this house through your eyes. You understand?' At her unwilling nod, he walked to his car and opened the passenger door. 'Shall we begin?'

At first Julia was as taut as a bowstring, wary of his proximity in the confines of the car, but as the tour proceeded, she began half unconsciously to relax, reassured by the fact that he seemed to need both hands for driving, and showed no disposition to lunge at her.

She had half expected to have to explain the workings of the estate in words of one syllable, but soon discovered her mistake. His questions were sharp and searching, revealing a keen and demanding intelligence. Julia had her work cut out to keep up with him, she discovered with no great pleasure.

Under his interrogation, in spite of herself, she began to talk about Ambermere, the way it had been in the past, the plans she had had for the future, her voice softening as she identified favourite landmarks, the places dear to her since childhood. Every hedge, every clump of trees seemed to have some deep and personal meaning, she realised with anguish, the eager spill of words choking in her throat.

He said, 'I think it is time we had something to eat. Can you suggest a place?'

Julia swallowed, grabbing at her composure. 'If

you take the left fork, it will bring you down to the lake. But you can drop me here. I should really be getting back to the house . . .'

'After we have eaten.' The words were quietly spoken, but the underlying note was implacable.

In the sunlight, the lake's waters gleamed like gold.

'It's something to do with the sediment,' Julia explained. 'And quite harmless. Fish thrive in it. And of course, it's how the house got its name.'

'Of course.' He handed her a rug. 'Spread this out, if you please, while I get the food.'

Nervously, Julia complied. She wished now that she had organised lunch for them at the house after all. A rug by the undoubted seclusion of the lake had all the connotations she most wanted to avoid. The dining-room at home would have been far less intimate, she thought, biting her lip.

The picnic hamper was a revelation. There was smoked salmon, and thick wedges of a creamy chicken pie, as well as salads, and crisp rolls. To follow there were nectarines, grapes, and thick, luscious strawberries, sprinkled with kirsch.

Julia's eyes widened, as she watched Alex Constantis deal effortlessly with the opening of a bottle of champagne.

'Isn't this all rather lavish for a simple day in the country?' she asked with a touch of sarcasm.

'You mean—rather vulgar?' He slanted a glance at her, as he handed her a glass. 'But what else could you expect from a peasant? Anyway, you forget I have a decision to celebrate.'

Julia's throat tightened. 'You're mistaken, Mr Constantis. I haven't forgotten a thing.'

'You are very formal.' He filled his own glass. 'Could you not bring yourself to call me Alex?'

'I think formality is preferable, under the circumstances.'

'As you wish.' He lifted his glass. 'Then let us drink together—to Ambermere, and its future.' He paused, seeing her hesitate. 'It does have one, I assure you, *thespinis.*'

Julia flushed slightly, then raised her glass in turn.

Silently he handed her a plate, cutlery, and a linen napkin, and they began to eat. In spite of her reservations, Julia found herself enjoying the food, and eating her full share of it. Being in the open air always sharpened her appetite, she thought ruefully, as Alex offered her a second helping of strawberries.

She shook her head and leaned back on her elbow, relishing the warmth of the sun, and the scent of the grass. If she'd been with anyone else, she thought ruefully, she would have been relaxed completely, having the time of her life. But Alex Constantis, even when playing the courteous host, as she could not deny he had done, was a menace to her peace of mind.

Aware that he was watching her, she hurried into speech. 'You speak very good English. Where did you learn it?'

His brows lifted slightly. 'I had an adequate education.' He paused, then added drily, 'Despite what you may have been told.'

'Told?'

Why, yes. Your father mentioned last night the vacation you had just enjoyed—the Embassy to which your uncle is attached. My cousin Paul has a posting to the same capital. I am sure you must have encountered him at some point. You are too beautiful for him to overlook.' His mouth twisted slightly. 'Nor could he have resisted telling you, as he tells everyone, how I robbed him of his supposed heritage. His mother and sister are equally voluble on the same subject.'

'You can hardly blame them,' Julia said bluntly. 'Usurpers are rarely popular.'

He laughed. 'So that is how you regard me,' he said, and there was a brief silence. At last he said, 'Hearing you talk about your home earlier was a revelation, Julia *mou*. You speak of it as a woman speaks of her lover.'

She looked down at her glass. 'Ambermere's been my life. I thought it always would be.'

He said laconically. 'And so it can.' He paused. 'If you marry me.'

Julia sat up with a jerk, spilling champagne on her shirt. She said unevenly, 'If that's a joke, it's in very poor taste.'

'Yet I am perfectly serious.' Alex reached across and removed the glass from her hand, setting it down at a safe distance. 'A house like Ambermere needs a woman, and my mother tells me it is time I was married.' The powerful shoulders lifted in a slight shrug. 'Maybe she is right.'

'So you propose to a woman you hardly know just because your mother thinks it's a good idea?' Julia managed a scornful laugh. 'Incredible!'

'Totally, if your premise were correct,' he agreed, unmoved. 'But we are not exactly strangers to each other, Julia *mou*.' He paused. 'Last night you asked me if I would give you Ambermere. Today I tell you—yes. But on my terms, not yours.'

'It's unthinkable!' Her voice sounded like a stranger's. 'I suppose you actually believe what that ghastly woman said. That I'd lend myself to such a disgusting—degrading arrangement—that I'd sell myself.' She scrambled up on to her knees, her small breasts heaving stormily. 'And to you,of all people!'

'Now why do you say that?' His voice was still mild, but there was a disturbing glitter in the dark eyes as they rested on her. 'Is my blood somehow unfit to mingle with yours?'

'It's nothing to do with that,' Julia returned defiantly. She took a deep breath. 'To be frank, Mr Constantis, you're not my type. In fact, you leave me cold.' She sent him a brittle smile. 'Not the way, I'm sure, you'd want your wife to feel.'

He picked a long blade of grass, brushing it meditatively across his chin as he surveyed her. 'It would cause difficulties, certainly. But is it, in fact, the case?'

He was taunting her, Julia realised furiously, needling her with a reminder of their shared memories of the previous night.

She said tautly, 'We're all guilty of uncharacteristic behaviour at times, Mr Constantis.' She shrugged, with an attempt at insouciance. 'Put mine down to too much alcohol—plus the fact that you took me by surprise.'

For a moment there was silence then Alex Constantis shrugged too, a graceful, half-humorous lift of the shoulders. He said softly, 'Then, if that is the only way, so be it.'

As he moved, Julia realised his intention and recoiled, sprawling backwards on to the rug as she did so.

As she tried to recover herself, Alex was there beside her, his body pinning hers to the ground, one hand capturing both her wrists and holding them above her head, rendering her helpless.

She said hoarsely, 'Let go of me, damn you!'

'Why?' The smile on his lips did not reach his eyes. 'What possible effect on you can this have?' He bent his head, brushing her lips almost negligently with his. 'Or even—this.' His free hand began to unbutton her shirt.

She said on a little moan of despair, 'No—oh God, no!' her body twisting and writhing as she sought to free herself.

He lifted himself slightly away from her, but only to thrust one lean, muscular thigh between hers.

He said, with a ghost of a laugh. 'Go on fighting me, *agapi mou*. I like it.'

The intimate pressure of his body against hers left her in no doubt as to what he meant, and embarrassment heightened the angry colour in her face.

'You swine!' she choked. 'You—you . . .'

'Bastard?' he jeered. 'Why don't you say it?' His fingers moved downwards, unhurriedly completing their task, and tugging the edges of her shirt aside.

She was wearing a bra today, but the fragile lace provided only a token covering, and Alex smiled in sensuous anticipation as he looked down at her. His hand found the small clasp in the valley of her breasts, and dealt with it expertly.

The breath caught agonisingly in her throat. The

sun dazzled her half-closed eyes, and in its centre he was total darkness as he bent towards her.

His fingers stroked one soft, pink-tipped mound, shaped it, held it for the caress of his lips. A whimper, half rejection, half need, rose in her throat as for the first time she felt his mouth against her naked flesh. A shaft of hot, shamed excitement pierced her body as his lips surrounded the engorged, rosy peak. His tongue circled her nipple languorously, playing with it, softly strumming the heated tip until the mingled pain and pleasure of it made her cry out, her body twisting again, but this time in the tumultuous unfamiliarity of abandonment.

He turned his head and began to kiss her other breast, and the warm, secret centre of her womanhood clenched in sharp delight, as she felt its aching reponse.

His hand moved down slowly, exploring her ribcage and the flat plane of her stomach, to the waistband of her jeans, and stopped. As if she was outside her own body, no longer in control, Julia felt her slender hips lift slightly, arching her, thrusting her against his imprisoning thigh.

Alex raised his head and looked down at her, his own breathing suddenly harsh and ragged, then with disconcerting swiftness he rolled away from her, and she was free.

For a long moment Julia lay still, her whole body throbbing as her paralysed mind tried to come to terms with what had happened to her.

From a thousand miles away, Alex's voice reached her softly, mockingly. 'If I leave you cold, Julia *mou*, then the man who can warm you is to be envied indeed.'

With a little choking gasp, Julia turned on her side away from him, trying to deal with recalcitrant clips and buttons with shaking, clumsy hands.

She couldn't believe what had just happened. How she had lain there and let him do that to her—and even wanted more. She wanted to leap to her feet and run away—to somewhere he would never find her—where she would never have to face him again.

A swift, humiliated glance over her shoulder revealed that he was repacking the hamper, his movements economical. It was clear that what had transpired had no means affected him in the same way, she realised wretchedly.

She had provoked him, and he had countered, and now she had to live with the knowledge that she had been his for the taking, she, the cool, the un-approachable.

Oh, God, she thought. It can't be true. It can't.

She looked up to find him standing over her, hands on hips. Dry-mouthed, she stared up at him, her hand shielding her eyes from the sun.

He said, 'Do you wish to go home?'

'I can find my own way.' Her voice sounded husky and unfamiliar.

She was sure he would argue, insist, but to her surprise he shrugged, carried the picnic things to the car, then climbed in and drove away.

She stayed where she was for a long time, staring unseeingly at the amber waters of the lake. Then eventually she got shakily to her feet and began to make her way towards the copse, where the gipsy trailers were parked. She had to see Grandma Pascoe again. There were things she wanted to ask her—things she had to know.

Ambermere, she thought, her nails scoring the soft palms of her hands—the Tower struck by lightning. And Alex Constantis—the King of Swords, coming to humble her. It was all mumbo-jumbo and coincidence, of course, but it was horribly, uncannily accurate at the same time.

And she wanted no more of it. She wanted the familiar comfort of handsome strangers, and unexpected windfalls.

But when she reached the copse she was aware of a strange stillness. She ran into the clearing and stopped, looking around her incredulously. It was empty. The trailers had gone, leaving the usual bare places on the grass, and the blackened patches where fires had been lit.

Julia cried out to the unheeding trees, 'But you can't leave me like this—you can't! You've got to take it all back—make things better.'

But only the silence answered. The Pascoes had gone, and heaven only knew when—or if—they would be back.

She walked home slowly, head down.

Safely in her room, she stripped and showered, letting the warm water teem down over the body she'd always taken so much for granted, and which had so totally betrayed her. She wanted to wash away the memories of Alex's hands—his mouth. To belong to herself again.

She dressed in old, familiar clothes—a wraparound skirt in a swirl of jade green, and a white blouse, square-necked and loose-sleeved. She brushed her damp copper hair until her scalp tingled, then tied it at the nape of her neck with a length of chiffon to match her skirt.

Julia Kendrick looked back at herself in the mirror with her usual composure, but the slow, subtle grind of frustration deep within her body told her it was a façade—a lie.

If he had stripped her naked—taken her—she would have made no move to stop him. She knew that, and it terrified her as nothing else—not even the loss of Ambermere—had ever done.

She'd been his—and he had been the one to draw back, to call a halt. That was what she now had to try to live with.

She stepped out on to the landing, nearly colliding with Mrs Parsons.

'I'm sorry, Madge.' She made herself smile, speak calmly. 'Were you looking for me?'

'You have a visitor, Miss Julia.' Mrs Parsons gave her an arch smile. 'I thought it was Sir Philip he'd come to see, but he asked for you instead.'

Hidden by her skirts, Julia's hands balled into tense fists, then relaxed. She maintained her cool, even though every instinct was warning her to run back into her bedroom and bar and bolt the door.

She didn't ask who it was. She knew already. Knew too why he was there. She went downstairs and across the wide hall to the drawing-room. Alex Constantis was standing near the fireplace. He had changed too, to the dark formality of a suit, and silk shirt and tie.

For an endless moment they stared at each other

across the room.

Then he said, with harsh abruptness, 'Will you marry me?'

Words of negation, of rejection filled Julia's brain, jostled each other for utterance.

From somewhere a long way outside herself, she heard her voice say, 'Yes.'

Alex nodded, a faint dull flush along his hard cheekbones. He said, 'I will speak to your father tomorrow.'

Then he walked past her to the door and was gone.

Julia fumbled her way to a sofa and sank down on to the cushions, trembling violently.

She thought, What have I done? Oh, God, what have I done?

CHAPTER FOUR

THEY WERE married three weeks later in a brief register office ceremony which spoke louder than words of her parents' total disapproval of her headlong decision.

Julia had never before faced such outright and prolonged condemnation of any of her actions, and she found the days preceding the wedding wretched and emotionally draining.

'You can't do this thing!' Lydia Kendrick had declared tearfully over and over again. 'You can't marry a man simply because you want to go on living in this house. It—it's obscene!'

And Julia replied wearily as she had done so many times, 'It isn't just the house . . .'

Lady Kendrick snorted. 'Then what else is it, pray? You can't pretend you're in love with that man—that upstart!'

No, Julia couldn't pretend that. She had no real idea what her feelings were towards Alex Constantis. And the devastating sensual impact that he'd made on her untried emotions was hardly something she could discuss with her mother, she thought ruefully.

By tacit consent, no public announcement had been made about their enagagement, although Alex had presented her with a ring—an exquisite star sapphire. He had handed it to her with a challenging lift of the brows, as if daring her to find it too large or too ostentatious, and she had thanked him with a quiet, 'It's beautiful.'

But he hadn't offered to place it on her finger, and most of the time Julia left the ring in its satin-lined box. The gift was a token to satisfy a convention, she thought, but it had no more significance than that, and certainly Alex, as she'd learned haltingly to call him, never demanded to know where it was.

And if her own feelings about this marriage were ambivalent, she had no idea at all about his. On the surface, he played the role of the attentive fiancé so skilfully that even Sir Philip and Lady Kendrick had no real criticism to level. He was civil, even charming, in the face of her mother's almost overt hostility. And he raised no objection at all to the wedding being little more than a hole-and-corner affair.

Julia herself was aware of a nagging disappointment. She had always envisaged herself standing at the altar in the small parish church, a vision in white silk chiffon, with family, friends and well-wishers crowding the pews.

She had imagined Alex himself wanting a full-dress ceremony too, to drive home to the locality and the world at large that although his own antecedents might be questionable, he was marrying into an old and respected family.

Yet he seemed totally uninterested in the details of how Julia was to become his wife. And the next shock had been to learn that not one member of his family would be attending the wedding.

'No one?' Julia had stared at him. 'But surely . . .'

'So who am I supposed to invite?' He had given

that characteristic shrug. 'My cousin Paul, who at the moment regards himself as my heir? His sister Zoe? My aunt Sophia?'

Julia had hesitated. 'But there's your mother.' She tried a smile. 'I haven't even met her yet and . . .'

'There is plenty of time for that.' He paused. 'My mother's health has not been good lately—she's had a virus—and a journey to England might tire her—apart from any other considerations,' he added with faint irony.

Julia had flushed. Alex was clearly concerned about the reception his mother might meet, and in all honesty she could not blame him. A simple Greek peasant woman could be destroyed by Lydia Kendrick's icy politeness.

But Alex's lack of supporters at the wedding was not the only surprise of the engagement.

Julia had assumed that once she had promised to be Alex's wife he would lose no time in pursuing his seduction of her to the ultimate conclusion. But, in fact, nothing could have been further from the truth.

He visited or telephoned her each day, of course, and on the two occasions when he had had to go abroad for a few days, he'd arranged for flowers to be sent.

His wooing of her, if that was what it was, had been conducted on strictly formal lines. He sought no opportunities to be alone with her, and when they were together he kept his distance. And his kisses were confined to the merest brushing of his mouth across her lips or cheek at arrival or leavetaking.

Julia had begun by being puzzled at his lack of

demonstrativeness, become angry, and then reverted to bewilderment again. She didn't want him to make love to her—that went without saying, she told herself defiantly—but at the same time his ability to remain aloof was a little disturbing, reminding her yet again how little she knew of the man she was going to marry.

Even more disturbing was her own reaction, each time she saw him or heard his voice on the telephone. She could neither deny nor defend the slow-burning excitement uncoiling inside her, but she could hide it, matching, on the surface at least, his coolness with her own. Although how far he was deceived it was impossible to say, she admitted ruefully. And no doubt he was supremely confident of his ability to sweep away all barriers between them on their wedding night, reducing her once more to the state of mindless passion she had experienced that day by the lake.

Well, that was the life he'd offered, and which she'd accepted, she thought with a little sigh. Mistress of his house by day, mistress of his body by night. She could hardly complain now of the starkness of the bargain between them.

But the thought of what it might mean to surrender completely to a man like Alex Constantis had come to dominate her thinking as the hours and minutes to her wedding ticked away.

Grandma Pascoe's warning that the King of Swords would humble her pride had returned to haunt her over and over again, much as she tried to dismiss it.

The night before her wedding day, she was prey to

swift, troublous dreams in which Ambermere became a house of empty, echoing rooms, through which she ran in an endless search—for what?

And as Philip Kendrick drove her, tight-lipped, to the register office in the nearby market town, Julia found herself wondering, with sudden chill, if Alex would even be there. That had been another of the previous night's dreams—finding herself, surrounded by curious eyes, waiting for a bridegroom who never arrived. Was that why he had invited no guests of his own to the ceremony—because he knew it would never take place?

Stop being ridiculous, she adjured herself almost frantically. Of course he'll be there. You're letting Grandma Pascoe's wild predictions get out of all proportion.

Alex was marrying her to provide himself with someone to run the house and estate he had acquired—and because he desired her, she reminded herself with a faint shiver. He had no reason to humiliate her publicly. She was letting her imagination run away with her.

Nevertheless, it was almost a relief to find him waiting there, with a tall, fair-haired man whom he introduced as Andrew Carstairs, his personal assistant in the UK.

Andrew Carstairs shook hands with Julia and her parents, and made appropriately genial comments, but it was clear he was no more impressed with this hasty, almost perfunctory marriage than the Kendricks themselves.

Within minutes, it seemed, it was all over, and Julia was driving back to Ambermere with her new husband. The wedding ring felt strange and heavy on her hand, she thought, twisting it round and round. She rarely wore jewellery, but this particular piece she would have to accustom herself to. She stole a sideways glance at Alex, but his shuttered expression gave no clue as to what he was thinking.

Apart from telling her that her simple white silk dress with its covering flower-embroidered jacket looked charming, and making his vows, he had said little, and the silence now between them in the car was beginning to prey on Julia, and make her nervous.

She said, 'A few of the neighbours are coming to have a drink, and wish us luck. I hope you don't mind.'

'Not at all, as long as their good wishes are not too prolonged. We have a plane to catch.'

They were flying to Athens, and joining Alex's yacht *Clio* at Piraeus, she knew, but their destination after that, he had told her, was a surprise.

Julia was not too concerned to solve the mystery. A cruise in the Aegean was no bad way to begin one's married life, after all, even if the marriage itself had not been made in heaven.

And when they returned, Sir Philip and Lady Kendrick would have moved to the temporary refuge of the Dower House, while negotiations were completed for the villa they were buying in the hills above Nice.

And Ambermere will be mine, Julia thought.

She was thankful, in the event, that the wedding reception had not been more formal or elaborate. Some of the congratulations were a little too hearty, as if the speakers were trying to convince themselves of their own sincerity. And she was aware of speculative looks behind the smiles.

Even Vivvy seemed slightly stunned that the one-time joke was a joke no more, and Julia was, in fact, Mrs Alexandros Constantis.

As soon as she could decently excuse herself, Julia went up to her room to put the few last items in her dressing case.

She was just checking the contents of her handbag when a sound from the doorway made her look round, and Tricia Bosworth strolled into the room.

'All alone?' She glanced around. 'I thought you might be closeted with Mummy, receiving some last-minute maternal advice on how to control men's baser animal instincts. Not that it'll do you much good,' she added with a faint shrug. 'No doubt you think you've been very clever—keeping Ambermere in the family, so to speak—but Alex Constantis will make you pay for the privilege, my dear, tonight, and every night. I only hope you don't find the price too high.' She giggled. 'Or is no sacrifice too great to make for Ambermere?'

Julia fastened the locks on her dressing case. 'None whatsoever,' she agreed serenely, aware that her colour had risen and longing to slap Tricia Bosworth across her sneering smile.

'Well, you've got guts, I'll grant you that.' Tricia sat down uninvited on the edge of the bed. 'So, do you plan to civilise your wild Hellene—turn him into an English country gentlemen? Or just smooth off the rougher corners a little?'

'I haven't decided yet,' Julia returned, maintaining

her composure with an effort.

'Of course,' Tricia went on, 'If you play your cards right, you don't need to see much of him at all. He can go off round the world, making money, and you can stay here, playing the gracious châtelaine, and spending it for him.'

'It sounds an ideal arrangement.' Julia found herself wondering almost dispassionately whether any other bride on her wedding day had been tempted to pick up the heavy silver-backed hand mirror from her dressing-table and smash it over a guest's head.

The important thing was not to show the least trace of irritation, and give Tricia Bosworth the petty victory she sought.

'Well, you seem to have it all worked out.' To Julia's relief, Mrs Bosworth rose, smoothing a none-existent crease out of her hyacinth-blue dress. She walked to the door, then turned, smiling. 'They say these Greek peasants are the most amazing studs. We must have a girls' get-together when you return from your honeymoon, and you can tell me if it's true.' She gave Julia a wink that managed to be both lascivious and conspiratorial, and departed.

Bitch, Julia thought, skaking with temper. Dirty-minded, evil-tongued bitch!

She sat down on her dressing stool, making herself breathe deeply, trying to relax. She couldn't go downstairs looking as she did, her eyes glowing with fury, and bright spots of colour burning on both cheeks.

The next rap on the door admitted Mrs Parsons. 'Mr Constantis asks if you're ready, Miss Julia—I mean Madam.'

'Quite ready.' It wasn't true. A host of butterflies were waging war somewhere in her midriff as she realised she was committed now—that there was no turning back.

And at the same time she was wondering why Alex had sent Mrs Parsons, instead of coming to tell her himself that it was time they left. Tricia Bosworth's lewd comments, although poisonous, had no foundation in fact, she though wryly. Alex had made no attempt even to kiss her so far, and the only time he had touched her was when he'd taken her hand during the ceremony itself. She supposed that as a nervous bride she should find his restraint reassuring—a sign of his consideration, but instead it made her uneasy. Was it reassurance—or simple indifference?

He knew he could make her want him when the time came, she thought, as she walked along the landing to the stairs in Mrs Parsons' bustling wake. Perhaps he'd decided that romancing his wife, making her feel special, was an unnecessary refinement to their relationship.

If so, it was a bleak prospect.

He was standing, obviously impatient, at the foot of the stairs, and Julia paused halfway down the broad flight, watching as he shot a glance at his watch, clearly not for the first time. Look at me, she heard herself begging silently. Smile at me. Hold out your arms, and I'll run to you.

When he did look up, she smiled down at him, tentatively, shyly, willing the dark face to soften, the hooded eyes to gleam with desire for her.

But he said abruptly, 'Say goodbye to your parents quickly, Julia. We are already running late.' And turned away, leaving her feeling, foolishly, as if she'd been slapped.

Julia leaned on the rail, watching the lights of Piraeus fade as *Clio* slid smoothly into the Saronic Gulf. Athens had been drily, enervatingly hot, and she had been grateful for the air-conditioning in the limousine which had taken them through the city and down, eventually, to the great bustling harbour.

She would have liked to linger, to extend her first look at the reality of Greece, but Alex had swept her inexorably on to the launch which was waiting to take them out to *Clio*.

Clio herself was a revelation. The stateroom to which Julia had been shown by an attentive white-coated steward was only marginally smaller than her bedroom at Ambermere, and completely dominated by a king-sized double bed. Julia had spent a couple of hilarious holidays sailing on the Solent with some boat-crazy friends, but the accommodation she'd enjoyed then was light years from this, she thought, blinking at the bathroom with its exquisite porcelain furniture and gold fittings.

But then being on board *Clio* was not like sailing at all. Julia was hardly aware of the yacht's motion, although the swarthy Captain Restaris, who had greeted them when they came on board, had warned that there might be a slight evening swell when they reached the open sea.

Julia lifted her face gratefully to the breeze. She still had no idea where they were going, she thought. Alex had been no more communicative on the plane than formerly. In fact, he'd immersed himself in papers produced from the briefcase which had accompanied him on to the plane. He'd apologised briefly for the necessity, it was true, but Julia had received the daunting impression that even if she'd protested, it would have made no difference. Not even the fact that it was his wedding day could deter Alex from overseeing the smooth running of the Constantis empire, she thought with a faint sigh.

But there was no doubt that he had her comfort in mind. She had been surprised to find waiting in her stateroom a slender, olive-skinned girl in a neat uniform who told her that she was Androula, come to wait on the *Kyria*. Julia had never had the services of a personal maid before, but it was pleasant to have her unpacking done for her, her bath run, and her clothes for dinner laid out ready.

And Androula's presence also had the effect of keeping Alex at bay, Julia realised rather ruefully. All the time she was dressing, and doing her hair and make-up, she had been on edge, expecting the door to open and admit him. But, once again, he had left her privacy undisturbed.

Nor were there any of his clothes or toiletries in her cabin, indicating that he had his own quarters elsewhere, although the satin sheets and twin lace-trimmed pillows reposing invitingly on the big bed seemed to demonstrate that he intended to sleep with her; but Julia was beginning to realise that with Alex it was unwise to take anything for granted.

In the meantime, there was dinner to get through. The steward Basilis had served her a cocktail in the big saloon, but she had felt conspicuous and out of place, being there alone, with no sign of Alex, and had made an excuse to take her drink up on deck.

Where she had remained ever since, she thought, with a slight grimace. *The Neglected Wife*—Act Two.

Surely Alex didn't intend to simply ignore her until—until bedtime? He couldn't be so unthinking—so cruel. Or could he? Had she already made too many assumptions about what being married to him would be like?

She heard a soft footstep behind her and tensed, but it was only Basilis come to tell her that dinner was served.

When she reached the saloon, Alex was waiting there, and she knew an absurd feeling of relief.

She said rather shyly, 'I've been up on deck. It's a beautiful evening.' She paused. 'Didn't Basilis tell you where I was?'

'Yes, but I had some work to finish.'

'And is it—finished, I mean?' Julia took her seat opposite him at the table and spread her napkin on her lap.

'Almost, I think. Why do you ask?' Alex filled her glass with wine.

Julia swallowed. 'Well, you seem to have been so occupied—I've seen so little of you . . .' Her voice trailed away into an embarrassed silence.

There was a silence, then he said drily, 'You flatter me, *agapi mou*. I had no idea you were so eager to be alone with me—to be the object of my—undivided attention.' He paused, the dark eyes running over her face and down to her shoulders and silk-veiled breasts in a caress as explicit as if he had reached out and touched her with his hand. 'But it will happen soon enough, I promise you.'

Julia bit her lip, feeling colour storm into her face. What was happening to her? That must have sounded as if she was begging for him to make love to her. And really, all she had wanted was some acknowledgement that she existed—that she mattered to him, even marginally.

Well, now she knew her exact standing in the scheme of things. When he had finished his paperwork, he would take her to bed. But while her mind, and her pride, recoiled in outrage from such cavalier treatment, she knew, to her shame, that her body was already responding with greedy anticipation to the prospect of his lovemaking.

Alex didn't have to humble her pride, she thought in self-derision. Where he was concerned, she had none.

The meal that Basilis served was delicious, but Julia tasted little of it, although she made an effort to eat.

Alex talked lightly on various topics, none of them personal, and Julia tried to follow his lead. There were a million questions she wanted to ask, but with Basilis always solicitously hovering, it was impossible. So perhaps it was better to chat about the Greek National Theatre, and the problems which the tourist boom had brought in its wake.

Besides, what could she say? 'Why did you marry me?' She bit her lip. That might be dangerous ground to cover—might bring an answer she did not want to hear.

But what would be the right answer—the answer she wanted him to give? That seemed equally dangerous to comtemplate.

When Basilis had served them small cups of thick, sweet coffee, he finally vanished.

Julia's mouth felt dry. She said haltingly, 'Your boat is fantastic. Like a floating palace.'

'It was built for my father. Since I came into my inheritance, I've used it a great deal. It has been my only real home.' He shrugged. 'There have been apartments—hotel suites, but they mean nothing.'

'And now you have Ambermere.'

'Yes, I have it.' He pushed his chair back and came round the table to her, pulling her out of her seat. 'And also, my beautiful one, I have you.'

For a long moment he looked at her, letting her see without evasion the open hunger in his eyes. Then he touched his fingers to his lips and put them gently, fleetingly on her mouth, before letting them slide down over her chin to the long line of her throat, and further down to the valley between her breasts, already aching for his touch, and still down over the clinging silk of her dress to the warm, moist joining of her thighs.

Julia gasped, her head falling back under the shock of his touch, as she realised the extent of her own need for him—and the power it gave him over her.

She said his name in a little cracked, imploring voice, her dazed eyes fixed on the firm line of his mouth. She wanted his lips on hers, longed for them, thirsted for them.

She heard him give a soft triumphant little laugh. 'Soon,' he said. 'Soon, *matia mou*, we will be together, alone, just as you want.' His hands moved to her hips, pulled her against him, so that for one agonising, dazzling moment their bodies ground together. Then he released her. 'Go now,' he told her quietly. 'Go to the cabin, and wait for me. I will come to you there.' As she turned half blindly towards the door, he added, 'And don't undress, Julia *mou*. I want that privilege for myself.'

The cabin had been prepared, she saw. The curtains had been drawn, and a lamp lit beside the bed, casting a softly intimate light. The covers had been turned down, and her white lace nightgown arranged across the bed in readiness. A basket of peaches had been placed on the bedside table, next to a bottle of champagne on ice. And there was fruit juice too in a tall frosted jug.

She was trembling and her mouth felt dry as she looked around her. The perfect setting, she thought, for a night of love. All that was lacking was her lover. 'Soon', he had promised, but every minute seemed an eternity.

She poured herself some of the fruit juice, and wandered round the cabin as she drank it, restless, unable to settle, her eyes fixed almost painfully on the door, as she waited for it to open.

What in the world could be keeping him away now? she asked herself, half in amusement, half in despair. He wanted her, so why wasn't he here with her now?

She poured some more juice and drank it, although she wasn't sure she cared for it overmuch. She didn't recognise the flavour, and there was an odd kind of aftertaste which lingered on her tongue. There was a quilted armchair beside one of the portholes, and she sat down in it, leaning back against the cushions, as the minutes ticked by.

She let her mind run back over the events of the day, remembering with a pang her mother's rigid face, and Tricia Bosworth's drawling malice. But she mustn't think of things like that now. She would prove to her parents and the world that she could make a success of her strange marriage.

She realised her eyelids were beginning to droop, and sat up with a jerk. If Alex didn't hurry, she would be asleep. She glanced at her watch and saw that she'd been waiting over half an hour.

He had told her not to undress, but she had to fight this drowsiness somehow. She got up from the chair, and swayed a little, putting a hand to her head. The stress of the wedding, the subsequent plane trip must have drained her more than she'd thought. Her head felt muzzy, and her eyelids seemed to have lead weights attached. She made her way, stumbling a little, to the bed, and sat down. The mattress felt as soft as a cloud, welcoming the weight of her body, and, sighing a little, she succumbed to the pleasure of complete relaxation.

She wanted to stay awake for Alex, but she was so sleepy—so desperately, inexplicably sleepy. She had to close her eyes—she just had to, and when Alex came, he would kiss her until she woke.

She was smiling as she drifted away into unconsciousness.

CHAPTER FIVE

SHE AWOKE to a fierce dazzling light. She opened her eyes slowly and wincingly, aware that her head was throbbing, and lay still for a moment, assimilating her surroundings with a sense of growing bewilderment.

She was no longer in her cabin on board the *Clio*. The bright light was sunshine, pouring in through an unglazed window, and reflected off the whitewashed walls of a small room.

She was lying on a hard, narrow bed, covered by a thin threadbare blanket, and as she moved, the springs protested clamorously.

Slowly and gingerly, Julia sat up. Under the blanket, she discovered with a sense of shock, she was naked. She looked round the room. Apart from the bed, there was little furniture, just a rickety chair, and a small chest with a domed lid. Nothing that she recognised, or which belonged to her. No personal possessions, and certainly no clothes.

Julia put her hands to her head, trying to remember, to make sense of this new situation. She had been waiting for Alex, she recalled, and she had dozed off. But that had been well before midnight, she thought, and judging by the position of the sun, it was now noon. Had she really slept all this time? And how in the world was she here, in little more than a hovel, when the previous night she had been wrapped in luxury on board the *Clio?*

Suddenly Julia began to be very frightened. She remembered an article she had once read about modern-day piracy. Had the *Clio* been boarded in the night, and had she been kidnapped—taken prisoner while she slept? If so, what had happened to Captain Restaris and the rest of the crew? And most important of all—where was Alex?

In one corner of the room was an open trapdoor, with a wooden staircase little better than a ladder leading down.

Julia sat up with determination, winding the blanket round her body like a sarong, before swinging her bare feet down on to the uneven concrete floor. She stood up, then sat down again abruptly, assailed by an oddly familiar dizziness.

And as she waited for her head to clear, she heard the sound of someone climbing the wooden stairs.

She looked wildly round for something with which to defend herself, but there was nothing but the chair, and she couldn't reach it in time. She shrank back towards the wall, the bedsprings providing an inharmonious accompaniment, as a man's dark head appeared through the trapdoor.

As she recognised him, Julia's lips parted in a soundless gasp.

'Alex!' Her voice cracked in relief. 'Oh, thank God! I've been terrified. What's happened? What are we doing here?'

'You have been asleep,' he said. 'And I have been waiting for you to wake up.' He took the chair and swung it round, sitting astride its seat, his arms resting on its back.

She looked at him remorsefully. It seemed she had denied them both their wedding night. 'Oh, Alex, I'm sorry.'

'Don't be,' he said. 'I intended that you should sleep.'

'You—intended?' Julia propped herself up on the single pillow and stared at him. Once again she remembered that awful debilitating drowsiness. She said slowly, 'The fruit juice—there was—something—in it?' Alex nodded, and she burst out, 'But why?'

He said laconically, 'Because I felt my plans for our honeymoon might not meet with your approval, and I wished to avoid an unnecessary scene.'

'I don't understand any of this.' Julia pushed her hair back from her face. 'Where's the *Clio*? And what's this awful place?'

'The *Clio* has gone,' he said. 'And this "awful place" '—he pronounced the words with open distaste—'happens to be the house where I was born.'

Julia bit her lip. 'I—I'm sorry,' she said awkwardly. 'I didn't realise. It was just such a shock to wake up and find myself—here.'

He nodded, the dark eyes watching her almost dispassionately. 'I meant it to be so.'

'You meant . . .?' Julia drew a deep breath. 'Alex, what's this all about? Why are we here, like this?'

'It is quite simple. You married a peasant, *kyria*. Now you are going to find out what life is like as a peasant's woman. It should prove—instructive, wouldn't you say?'

There was a silence. Julia put a hand to her head.

'Is this some kind of joke?'

'No.'

'You expect me to spend my honeymoon here—in this house?'

'I expect more than that.' He began to tick off on his fingers. 'You will clean for me, and you will cook, and wash my clothes, and tend the garden. You will feed the chickens, and also milk the goat.'

'I'll do nothing of the sort!' Julia sat up energetically, grabbing at her blanket as it began to slip. 'Have you gone mad? I'm your wife, not some kind of domestic slave, and . . .'

'No,' he said, 'you are not my wife. Not yet. You are the woman with whom I went through a ceremony of marriage. But you belong neither in my bed nor in my heart.'

Her throat felt suddenly constricted. 'What do you mean?'

'I was so easy to dazzle, *ne*? Or so you thought. The vulgar Greek peasant—the usurper of the family fortune. All names that you called me—showing your contempt for me. But when you found I wanted your house, that was different. You decided to sacrifice yourself—the well-born English rose and the rough Greek.' He smiled without humour. 'There is a story, is there not, of Beauty and the Beast? Is that how you saw me, Julia *mou*? As a beast you could tame? You despised me, but you thought you could manipulate me and my money to provide the life you wanted.'

'No!' Julia shook her head, her eyes widening with shock. 'No, that's not true . . .'

'You married me for a house,' he interrupted inexorably. 'Well, *matia mou*, I make you a gift of this one. It is not as—stately—as Ambermere, but it will serve, until you learn your place.' His mouth curled as he looked at her. 'And as I do not want you as a wife, then a "domestic slave", to use your own quaint phrase, you must be.'

'Alex, you don't—you can't mean this! It's our honeymoon. I know I shouldn't have said those things to you, and I'm sorry, but it was a long time ago, and in the heat of the moment. I was upset about losing Ambermere—surely you see that? But everything's changed now—we're married.' She swallowed. 'And—I—I need you.'

'Do you?' He laughed softly, but there was an underlying note which chilled her. 'Then, as you once said to me, *agapi mou*—eat your heart out.' He swung himself lithely up from the chair and pointed to the domed chest. 'You will find some clothes in there. Dress yourself, and come down, and I will explain your duties.'

'Alex!' As he began to turn away, Julia knelt up on the bed, deliberately letting the blanket slip down below her breasts. 'Alex, you can't mean this.' She swallowed. 'Don't you want me—just a little?'

The dark eyes flicked over her without emotion. 'Of course,' he said. 'You are very lovely, as I discovered last night when I took the clothes from your body with my own hands. But there is no respect between us, Julia, and without respect there can be no marriage.' He threw his head back, the dark eyes glittering coldly at her. 'You are spoiled and proud, and there is no beauty in that. If you are ashamed of me—of what I was—then that is your problem. While you are here, you will learn to solve it.'

'And if I don't?' She still couldn't believe this was really happening.

'Then the marriage will be annulled. I will not take a women who despises me, or who thinks she can use me for her own selfish purposes. So cover yourself or not as you wish. It makes no difference.'

He stepped down on to the top rung of the stair, and vanished.

Julia collapsed back on the bed, huddling the blanket around her. In spite of the heat, she felt deathly cold, and a slow, scalding tear ran down the curve of her cheek.

This couldn't be real. It couldn't! It was another of those awful dreams, and presently she would wake on board the *Clio* wtih Alex's arms around her.

But no nightmare, however potent, could have invented this awful squeaky bed with its hard, lumpy mattress, or the blanket scratching at her naked skin. There was a terrible reality about all these things—and about the way Alex had looked at her—the things he'd said.

Wincing, she remembered some of the words she had used to him, and about him. If she was honest, he had every right to be angry, and her parents' attitude to him over the past weeks had simply compounded the injury.

But that didn't mean she was going to tamely submit to being treated like this.

I'll talk to him, Julia thought. Reason with him. Make him see that he's wrong about me. Make him know that I want him, that I'm proud to be his wife.

She got off the bed and trod cautiously over to the chest, wondering what clothes he had brought for her to wear. Unless he had allowed Androula to do the packing, he had probably chosen all the wrong things. She hoped he had included some of those pastel cotton jeans and tops.

When she lifted the lid, she stayed very still for a moment, staring down at the chest's contents. These weren't her things—any of them. There were a couple of dresses, one dark red, the other a muddy shade of green, both clean but desperately shabby. There was a headscarf, and a pair of cheap plastic sandals. And that was it.

Julia turned the pathetic pile of garments over, her hands shaking. Nothing from her trousseau—none of the pretty leisure clothes and romantic evening silks and chiffons. Not even a pair of her own shoes—or a bra and brief set.

'Aren't you ready yet?' This time she hadn't heard his approach up the ladder, and she spun round with a little cry.

'I'm not ready, nor am I likely to be.' She pointed into the chest. 'These are not my clothes.'

'Consider them a loan.'

'I wouldn't consider them for a jumble sale,' Julia said coldly. 'I'd like my own things, please.'

'Still so imperious,' Alex said calmly. 'But you will learn.'

'I doubt that. Where are my clothes?'

'On board the *Clio*.' He paused. 'And many miles from here.'

Julia assimilated this. 'You really mean she's sailed without us? I don't believe you.'

'Go and look for yourself.'

She gave him a mutinous look. 'Without clothes?

How can I?'

'There are clothes there for you. 'Not, admittedly, what you have been accustomed to, Julia *mou*, or what you hoped I would provide for my wife, but adequate.'

'Apart from one major omission. You forgot to include any underwear.'

He shrugged. 'The weather is warm, and the dresses will cover you well enough.'

Julia stared at him. 'You actually think that I'm going to walk about in front of people wearing nothing but a dress and a pair of sandals? Well, I'm damned if I . . .'

'Calm yourself.' He did not raise his voice, but she heard the warning note plainly enough. 'There is no one to see you but myself.'

'No one . . .' Julia stopped, and drew a breath. 'Why not? What is this place?'

'It is an island called Argoli,' he said. 'No one lives here any more. We are totally, completely alone, *agapi mou.*' He paused, then added mockingly,' Just as you wished us to be.'

'Did I say that?' Julia flung back at him. 'I must have been out of my mind! And I still don't believe any of this.'

Stumbling a little over the trailing blanket, she went over to the window and leaned out. 'There's a street,' she said. 'And houses. And I can see a church . . .'

'All empty. The villagers moved to the mainland five years ago. One day I hope to provide some kind of industry to tempt them back, but until that time, their absence makes this place ideal for my purpose.'

Julia craned her neck in the opposite direction, catching a glimpse of azure sea. Slowly she drew herself back into the room. She didn't have to go and check on the *Clio*; she knew that it would not be there. She was here, it seemed, for the duration, with a man intent on his own unique revenge for the slights he had suffered at her hands.

Alex said, 'Put this on,' and tossed the red dress at her feet. He paused. 'Unless you want me to dress you.'

Julia faced him, lifting her chin challengingly. 'Yes,' she said, 'I do.'

Alex shrugged, then bent and retrieved the dress from the floor. As impersonally as if he was changing a dummy in a department store window, he stripped the blanket from her and threw it on to the bed, before tugging the dress, not altogether gently, over her head, turning her so that he could pull the zip up. Even when fastened, the dress hung on her like a tent. Glancing down at herself, Juila didn't know whether to laugh or cry.

'Do you wish me also to put on your shoes, or can you manage those yourself?' Alex jibed.

He couldn't have demonstrated his indifference to her, naked or clothed, more plainly, Julia thought wearily. She bent her head. 'I can manage.'

'Good,' he said. 'Then come downstairs. You have a meal to prepare.'

'I can't cook,' she protested. It wasn't strictly true. She could manage omelettes, beans on toast and other snacks, but living at home with Madge Parsons reigning as queen of the Ambermere kitchen, there had been no incentive to improve her culinary skills.

'Then you will learn. Or you will be very hungry.'

Unwillingly Julia put on the sandals and followed him

through the trapdoor. 'And if I fall off these stairs and break my neck, I suppose there's no hospital here either?'

'If you break you neck, Julia *mou*, I doubt whether a hospital can help you. I advise you to take care.'

And he didn't just mean on the stairs either, Julia realised wretchedly.

She stood and looked round the downstairs room with a sinking heart. It was just as unsophisticated as the bedroom, if not more so.

There was an ancient blackened stove, still filled with ashes which looked as if they'd been there since Homer was a lad. There was a square table in the middle of the room, covered with chipped Formica, and flanked by two folding plastic chairs. There was a strictly functional camp bed in the corner where Alex, presumably, had spent the night. And there was a sink bowl resting starkly in a sturdy wooden frame, its downpipe leading out through the wall below the window being its sole concession to modernity.

Julia swallowed. 'There aren't any taps,' she heard herself say.

'There is no running water,' came the equable reply.

'Then how on earth . . .?'

'There is, however, a bucket,' Alex went on briskly, as if she hadn't spoken at all. 'In which *yineka mou*, you may fetch water from the well in the street. For drinking purposes, there is also a spring at the back of the house.'

'And that's it?' Julia looked at him in frank disbelief.

'As you say,' he agreed laconically.

'Oh, this is impossible—a joke!' Julia sat down on one of the plastic chairs.

'I hope you will still be laughing at the end of the day.' He paused. 'I sugggest you begin by lighting the stove.'

'That thing? Does it still work?'

'I hope so. The Japanese enjoy raw fish in their diet. You, I think, would not.'

'And nor would you,' Julia returned defiantly. 'So, if the stove won't light, we'll have to declare a truce, and return to civilisation.'

'Oh, no, *matia mou.*' As he shook his head, Alex's smile did not reach his eyes. 'Because the stove will light perfectly well, with sufficient kindling. So do not try to play games, or you will be sorry.'

Their glances met and clashed, and it was Julia, to her shame, who looked away first.

He was completely mad, she told herself, but the madness would pass. He might have been brought up in this discomfort and squalor, but that didn't mean he had to like it. Everything about Alex Constantis spoke of him enjoying the good things in life, so this sojourn on Argoli had to be as much a penance for him, as for her.

Making me miserable is one thing, she thought. Punishing himself at the same time is another. I give this—horror—two days at the outside. And in the meantime I'll have to humour him.

She got to her feet and walked through the open door into the sunshine beyond, pausing for a moment, her hand shading her eyes, to get her bearings.

Away to her left, the village street sloped downwards between the sparse and empty houses, and behind them neglected olive groves shimmered in the heat, their leaves like silken, silver canopies. Beyond that, there seemed to be little but bare rock, stretching upwards towards the stark, unsullied blue of the sky.

Utter desolation, Julia thought with a shiver, just like the emotional morass inside her. She found her hands had clenched into shaking fists, relaxed with an effort, and walked round to the rear of the house.

There had once been a fair-sized garden scratched here in the red and dusty earth, but it was now overgrown with weeds, although the chickens Alex had mentioned were pecking fervently in the undergrowth. In the distance, the promised goat grazed in the shade of a gnarled olive tree.

Julia bit her lip, as she turned away and surveyed her immediate surroundings. There was nothing to lift the heart here either. Some rusting oil drums, a mangle with wooden rollers which looked as if it belonged in an industrial museum, and a few new-looking bags of sand and cement. There was also a small hut. Julia glanced inside, and recoiled. These were clearly the usual offices, so beloved of English estate agents, although there was little usual about a hole in the ground with a crumbling concrete surround, she thought, shuddering.

She took another long look around her, then turned back to the house, stopping with a little cry as she realised Alex had followed her, and was standing a few yards away, hands on hips, surveying her enigmatically.

'So, how do you like your new estate, Julia *mou*?' The underlying sneer was quite palpable. Probably he expected her to throw herself on her knees at his feet, babbling for mercy.

She lifted her chin. 'It's—basic,' she acknowledged coolly. 'I'm still looking for the woodpile.'

'Then you will look for a long time. On Argoli, if you want wood, you collect twigs and fallen branches where you find them.' He waved a hand towards the sheltering olive trees. 'Good hunting.'

'Now just a minute!' Julia exploded. 'You actually expect me to go scavenging for wood in this heat . . .?'

The dark brows snapped together menacingly. 'I have already told you what I expect. Do not make me repeat myself.'

'Oh, forgive me,' she bit back. 'And while I'm—hewing wood, and drawing water in the old tradition, what will you be doing, exactly? After all, there's no taverna here for you to sit in and—gossip, and gamble with the other men. Isn't that how the division of labour goes round here?'

Alex shrugged. 'If that is what you choose to think,' he returned coolly. 'But don't worry *matia mou*, I shall be well occupied. I have our food to provide, for one thing. I hope you like fish,' he added with a trace of mockery.

'I suppose I have no choice,' Julia said stonily.

'Now you begin to understand at last.'

Sudden inspiration came to her. 'But if we're really the only people here, where did the chickens come from—and that bloody goat? They don't look as if they've been starving here since everyone left.'

'The goat's name is Penelope,' he told her softly. 'And I suggest you make a friend of her, Julia, if you wish to have milk while you are here. But you are right, of course. They are as new to Argoli as yourself. I had them imported specially.'

'You must have been planning this for a long time.' Julia's voice was husky.

'Oh, yes.' Alex gave a meditative nod. 'Since the moment I decided to marry you, Julia *mou*, instead of taking you as my mistress.'

The sheer arrogance of him had her reeling. She said thickly, 'You think—you actually think I would have done such a thing?' She threw back her head, and laughed. 'You should have stuck to your original scheme, *kyrie*. I could simply have slapped your face and walked out of your life, sparing myself—this ridiculous farce.'

His mouth curled. 'How you cling to your illusions, *agapi mou!* From the time we met, I could have taken you at any time, and you know it, if you have a breath of honesty anywhere in that delectable body. All during our engagement you were wondering why I didn't kiss you—touch you as you wanted me to. Every smile, every look, every word told me you couldn't wait to sleep in my bed. And I was tempted, believe me,' he added with faint self-derision. 'But other considerations prevailed.'

'Your even more burning desire to humiliate me.' Her voice shook.

'When you agreed to be my wife, you chose to share my life,' he said with a shrug. 'At the moment my life is here, and you will learn what it means to live it.' He gave her a level look. 'Learn quickly, Julia *mou*, and the lesson will soon be over.' He paused. 'Now go and find your wood—but wear your headscarf,' he added warningly. 'You are not used to the fierceness of the sun here.'

She said between her teeth, 'Heatstroke would be a welcome alternative to your plans for me, believe me.'

'Another illusion,' he said lightly, but his eyes never left hers. 'Accept the first part of your schooling, Julia. Learn to obey me.' He added starkly, 'If you fight me, you will lose, and you will find the consequences truly humiliating, I promise.'

'Meaning that you'll beat me, I suppose!' Julia said with contempt. 'How truly macho! Unfortunately for you, there are laws now against behaviour like that, even towards your wife.'

'But unfortunately for you, *agapi mou*, no laws operate here but my own,' he said almost silkily. 'And there are other ways of punishing a recalcitrant woman than taking a stick to her.' He paused, his brows lifting. 'You wish, perhaps, to discover some of them?'

Tension seemed to envelop them. Julia could feel it crouching in the air like a distant storm. She wanted to call his bluff, but for a piercing, terrifying inner conviction that he wasn't bluffing at all.

She bit back the hot, defiant words crowding to her lips. She had a war to win. She couldn't afford to lose a first, and possibly decisive battle.

'No.' She swallowed. 'I—I'll do as you say.'

'Very wise.' Alex glanced at his watch. 'I will be back in just over an hour. I shall expect to find at least coffee keeping hot on the stove when I return. You will find any supplies you need in the store cupboard beside the sink.' He gave her a faint smile. 'And do not waste time trying to think of ways to escape, *agapi mou*. Except for a few lizards, we are alone here.' His smile widened. 'An idyll, *ne*—if not the kind you once expected to share with me.'

He walked away, and disappeared round the side of the house. By the time Julia could force her shaking legs to follow, there was no sign of him.

She stood alone in the deserted street and listened to the silence. In spite of herself, she wanted crazily, desperately to call his name, bring him back to her side if only for a moment.

'Oh, God,' she said aloud, her voice bitter. 'You fool! You stupid, pathetic, weak-kneed—idiot!'

She couldn't still want him—not a man who could treat her with the kind of callous contempt Alex had displayed. A man who didn't care for her—who didn't even desire her enough to mitigate his need to revenge himself on her. And even if he did—relent eventually—what hope, what future could there be in such a relationship?

Julia lifted her face to the burning, alien sky and felt the first heavy, scalding tears emptying down her face.

CHAPTER SIX

THE HOUR that followed seemed to Julia to encompass several lifetimes.

Cleaning out the stove had been a major operation, the flying dust and ash stinging her eyes and nose, and clinging to her hair and perspiring skin.

And she couldn't delude herself that the armfuls of wood that she'd collected and carried awkwardly back to the house were going to last even the rest of the day. The stove seemed to have a voracious appetite, or maybe she just hadn't discovered the knack of regulating it yet.

Oh, let it be that! she thought longingly.

Nor could she have dreamed how back-breaking the simple task of hauling up a bucket of water on a rope could be. She seemed to have spilled half the precious load over her feet, as she struggled back up the street, her arm muscles protesting at the unexpected weight they were supporting.

But she had managed to heat a pan of water almost to boiling point on the stove, and had found a big jar of instant coffee in the cupboard Alex had indicated, as well as a couple of thick enamel mugs.

He'd spoken as if they would live only on fish, but the cupboard had also contained a plentiful supply of tinned food. Rather too plentiful, Julia decided with a private grimace. It was clear she wasn't going to be let off lightly with just a token segregation here.

In a lean-to building on the other side of the house she had found gardening implements, and tools, as well as a sack of potatoes, and a fair supply of charcoal, to be used, she supposed, for grilling food under the cast-iron grid at one side of the stove.

Now Julia sat limply at the table, staring into space. She had somehow to find a way of getting out of this lunatic situation. She couldn't endure another day like this.

But it was useless to hope that Alex might relent. He was clearly intent on grinding her into the dust, she thought miserably, just as Grandma Pascoe had predicted.

Uncouth barbarian, she thought. His cousin Paul doesn't know the half of it. Yet, shameful though it was, she couldn't deny the physical attraction that still existed between them. That had been there from the first, outraging every cherished belief in her own fastidiousness—her ability to remain aloof, to flirt lightly at a distance. Alex had swept them away the first time he had touched her, she thought bitterly, remembering his taunt about her 'illusions'.

She was certainly deluding herself if she thought she could disguise her unguarded, almost greedy response to his lovemaking. When he'd claimed she had been his for the taking, he'd spoken no more than the truth, reluctant though she might be to admit it.

The only comfort she could cling to, she thought wearily, was that Alex had made it clear he was no longer interested in her body, But the realisation that his contempt for her outweighed any desire he'd ever felt for her was somehow the greatest humiliation of all.

She should be glad he didn't want her, she told herself fiercely. This way, it was easier to hate him for what he was doing to her.

She swallowed. While he kept her at arms' length, she was safe. The problem would be if and when Alex decided to make their marriage a real one. Could she yield her body to him without surrendering her emotions as well? Or wouldn't it be better to cut her losses from the start—ask him for the annulment he had already mentioned as a possibility?

'Why are you sitting there? Why haven't you cleaned up the house yet?' Alex's voice cut harshly across her reverie, and she jumped.

'I lit the stove.' It was an effort to reply normally. 'And the coffee's ready.'

'So I should hope,' he said grimly. 'I see you have managed to cover most of the room with ash as well as yourself. Before you sit and rest, you clear up the mess you have made.' He went outside for a moment, returning with a sweeping brush which he tossed to her. 'Here.'

Helplessly Julia watched him put a heaped spoonful of coffee in a mug, and add boiling water, before taking the drink and one of the chairs out under the sagging porch roof which fronted the house.

She discovered she wanted to burst into tears, and gritted her teeth instead.

'Beast!' she muttered through them. 'Brute!' And, as she began awkwardly and inefficiently to sweep the dirty floor, 'Bully!'

It seemed to take for ever, and she couldn't believe

it looked much better when she'd finished, she thought, sighing.

When she had finished, her throat felt as if it was coated in grit. Her thirst for coffee had disppeared completely. All she wanted now was some cool water, she thought, dipping the other mug into the bucket.

She raised it to her lips, but before she could drink it was snatched away.

Alex said, his voice molten with anger, 'You do not drink water from the well unless it has been boiled, you fool of a girl! Did I not tell you? Water for drinking comes only from the spring.'

'I forgot,' Julia said defiantly. 'And surely it wouldn't matter just once?'

'It might matter very much,' he said impatiently. 'Now come with me.'

His hand gripped her arm as he walked her up through the grove of olive trees, past the tethered goat with her mild curious face to the place where water gushed out of the bare rock, cold and crystal clear.

'I didn't bring the mug!' Julia wailed.

'Use your hands—like this,' Alex demonstrated, cupping his palms beneath the small torrent. He would have allowed the water to run away again, but Julia gripped his wrists.

She said huskily, 'Please . . .' and bent her head to drink from his hands.

For a brief second he was motionless, then he muttered something harsh and violent in his own language, freeing himself without gentleness, letting the water spill. His fingers twisted into her hair,

pulling her up to face him. There was anger in his
eyes and a heated flush along his cheekbones as he
said, 'Make your own cup, girl.'

He turned and strode away from her, back towards
the house. Julia remained where she was, staring
after him. Just for a moment, she thought slowly, she
had seen him affected by the intimacy of her action.
She had seen him vulnerable. It was hardly a
breakthrough, but it proved she still had a weapon
she could use against him.

She cupped her hands and drank, cupped and
drank, until the burning in her throat had subsided,
then she let the icy water trickle over her wrists and
hands, before splashing handfuls on to her grateful
face. Murder on the complexion, she thought, but
who cares?

When she got back to the house there were two fish
lying on the table, with a knife beside them, Alex was
lighting some charcoal beneath the grill.

'Supper?' Julia averted her gaze from the two pairs
of dead eyes which seemed to be staring at her. 'Poor
things!'

'You would prefer to go hungry?' His voice was
cool.

'No, but there's plenty of tinned stuff.'

'That is for emergencies—when the fish do not
bite,' he told her with a touch of grimness. 'Now,
clean and prepare them. And be careful—the knife is
sharp.'

It looked positively lethal, Julia thought,
swallowing. 'You said—clean them?'

He glanced round at her. 'Is there some problem?'

She tried to speak lightly. 'A small one. I've never

—actually dealt with a fish—before its arrival in the dining-room, that is.'

Alex got to his feet, dusting his hands on the faded jeans which, she had already noticed, fitted him like a second skin.

'Your domestic gifts are pitifully few, *yineka mou,*' he remarked with faint grimness. 'I suppose I should be grateful you can boil water.' He came to the table, and picked up the knife. 'Now watch.'

Julia obeyed, her face twisted into a grimace as she observed the swift expert movement of the knife, then saw with horror that he was presenting its handle to her.

'Now it is your turn,' he told her.

'Mine?' She bit her lip. 'I don't think I can.'

'And I say you must.' His voice was implacable. 'Do you wish to spend the rest of your life as a useless ornament, *pedhi mou?*'

'This has probably been the least ornamental day I've ever spent,' Julia said wearily, taking the knife from him.

Five minutes later she looked down at the mangled result of her efforts.

'That will be yours,' was Alex's only comment.

She supposed she'd asked for that. Under his tight-lipped guidance, she put the fish carefully on the grille above the glowing charcoal, and sprinkled them with seasoning, herbs and olive oil.

While the fish were cooking, Alex showed her how to make a salad, Greek style, with chopped cucumbers and enormous tomatoes, black olives and slices of *feta* cheese, the whole thing dressed with more of the thick, tangy green olive oil, and a squeeze

4 BOOKS PLUS A CLOCK AND MYSTERY GIFT

Here's a sweetheart of an offer that will put a smile on your lips . . . and **4 FREE** Mills & Boon Romances in your hands. **Plus** you'll get a digital quartz clock and a mystery gift as well.

At the same time, we'll reserve a Reader Service subscription for you. Every month you could receive 6 brand new Mills & Boon Romances by leading romantic fiction authors, delivered direct to your door. And they cost just the same as the books in the shops — postage and packing is always completely FREE. There is no obligation or commitment — you can cancel your subscription at any time. So you've nothing to lose! Simply fill in the coupon below and send this card off today.

Please send me 4 FREE Mills & Boon Romances and my FREE clock and mystery gift.
Please also reserve a Reader Service subscription for me. If I decide to subscribe, I shall receive 6 brand new Romances each month for £7.50, post and packing free. If I decide not to subscribe I shall write to you within 10 days. The free books and gifts will be mine to keep in any case.

I understand that I may cancel my subscription at any time by simply writing to you. I am over 18 years of age.

9A8T

NAME_____

ADDRESS_____

_____

_____POST CODE_____

The right is reserved to refuse an application and change the terms of this offer. Overseas please send for details. You may be mailed with other offers as a result of this application. Offer expires March 31st 1989.

AS A READER SERVICE SUBSCRIBER, YOU'LL ENJOY A WHOLE RANGE OF BENEFITS. . .

This attractive digital quartz clock — Yours Free!

* ★ Free monthly newsletter packed with competitions, recipes, author news and much, much more.
* ★ Special offers created just for Reader Service subscribers.
* ★ Helpful friendly advice from the ladies at Reader Service. You can call us any time on 01-684-2141.

So kiss and tell us you'll give your heart to Mills & Boon.

--------✂--

RUSH

**Reader Service
FREEPOST
P.O. Box 236
Croydon, Surrey
CR9 9EL**

POST THIS CARD TODAY!

NO
STAMP
NEEDED

of juice from a lemon she was sent to pick from the tree in the next garden.

'That looks wonderful.' In spite of her struggle with the fish, the smell of them cooking was making her mouth water, reminding her how long it was since her last meal.

She couldn't help remembering the saloon on *Clio*, the immaculately laid table with its shining silver and spotless linen, and contrasting it with her present surroundings.

'Well, make the most of it,' warned Alex. 'The fresh food will not last for ever.'

Julia's eyes widened when he produced a bottle of golden wine, and opened it.

'Retsina,' he told her. 'Have you tasted it?'

She shook her head. 'I've had ouzo, of course.'

He poured some of the wine into a tumbler and handed it to her. 'Try it.'

Julia sipped, and choked. 'My God, what's that taste?'

'Resin from the casks it's stored in.' Alex looked amused. 'Is it too strong for you? It is an acquired taste.'

'I thought it was part of the punishment—that you were trying to poison me.' She put the glass down on the table.

'Why, no, *agapi mou*,' There was a grin in his voice. 'My vengeance will not be accomplished so quickly—or so finally.'

'Thank you,' said Julia with irony.

The appearance of her fish hadn't improved while it was cooking, but its freshness and flavour were superlative, and she finished every morsel.

For dessert, to her surprise, Alex produced some grapes, explaining that there was a vine grown wild elsewhere in the village. The grapes were large, slightly sharp, and utterly delicious, and Julia felt replete when she had finished her bunch.

She said, 'That was a marvellous meal.' She leaned back in her chair, yawning. In spite of her enforced sleep the previous night, she was genuinely tired again. All the unaccustomed exertion, she told herself wryly.

'Tomorrow it will be your responsibility.' During the meal, the atmosphere had relaxed slightly, but now Alex's voice was brusque again. 'And you cannot sleep yet, Julia *mou.*'

She looked across the table at him, smiling, lashes lowered demurely. So she hadn't been mistaken, she thought exultantly. He did want her, after all. 'No?' Her voice sounded suddenly husky.

'You have to wash up, and tidy the room.'

If he'd picked up the bucket and tipped the remaining cold water over her head, she couldn't have felt more—quenched.

She said, 'Of course. I'd better heat some more water.'

The sun was setting as she finished, but the air was still warm, without a breeze. Julia pushed her hair out of her eyes, and thought longingly of her turquoise-tiled bathroom at Ambermere.

When Alex came in for the coffee she'd made, she said, 'I wish there was a shower.'

'There is a bath,' he said. 'Shall I fetch it for you?'

She guessed what it would be like, and she was

right. It was galvanised, and practical in the extreme, permitting the bather to sit, knees to chin, or stand. But it was better than nothing.

There was a domed chest beside his bed, similar to the one upstairs, and Alex delved in this to produce a rough towel and a new bar of soap.

'Luxury,' she said, with irony.

He put the soap and towel down on the table, and turned to the door. He said harshly, 'Do not take too long.'

In a voice she barely recognised as her own, she said, 'Won't you stay—and wash my back?'

Alex swung round, and looked at her. 'Is that—truly what you want, *agapi mou?*'

'Yes,' she said unsteadily, knowing with a pang of self-disgust that it was no more than the truth. 'Oh, Alex, yes. . . '

He shrugged. 'Alas,' he said, 'it has been a day of disappointments for you, has it not?' He walked out of the door, leaving her alone.

The water was barely tepid, but Julia revelled in the feel of it on her skin, in spite of the ache of frustration deep inside her. She soaped and rinsed every inch of her body, feeling some of her weariness ease as she did so. She washed her hair too as best she could. When she had finished, she wrapped herself in the towel and dragged the bath with some difficulty to the door to empty it. Once again Alex seemed to have vanished off the face of the earth.

Not a very large earth, Julia thought, as she put the bath away. Only a few miles long, and even fewer wide. He couldn't be that far away.

She had twisted her hair up on to the top of her head,

and now she shook it free, sighing soundlessly. It was all very well telling herself he'd gone for a long walk because he was aching himself, but the fact was she had been rejected again.

I'm going to have to stop leading with my chin, she told herself ruefully.

In the meantime, the bath had relaxed her enough to make her ready for what passed for a bed upstairs. Carrying her dress and sandals, she climbed slowly up the wooden steps.

A thin moon had risen and was framed in her window. It was unlucky to see a new moon that way, she thought hazily, but how much worse could everything get anyway?

She put the dress down on the chest, with her sandals beside it, then climbed on to the bed, pulling the sheet over her, grimacing as the mattress groaned at her.

She was almost asleep when she heard his footstep on the stair. She sat up immediately, propping herself on her elbow, staring across the shadowed room at him, her mouth suddenly dry.

Alex said softly, 'So you are awake.' As she watched, he peeled off the shirt he was wearing and let it drop to the ground. It was the first time she had seen him even partially stripped, and her widening eyes flicked achingly, yearningly over the broad, muscular shoulders and strong hair-roughened chest, The dark hair grew in a vee down over his stomach, and disappeared into the waistband of his jeans.

Stunned, Julia watched him unzip the jeans and push them down over his hips. He dropped them on to his shirt, and followed them with the dark briefs that were his last remaining covering.

She had never seen a man naked before, except in pictures and sculpture, and Alex could have modelled for any of them, she realised. He was—beautiful, his body lean, magnificent and totally virile.

She stared at him without shame, filling her eyes with him, wanting him with sharp completeness.

He reached out a bare foot and touched the pile of clothes.

'Laundry,' he said quite gently. 'For the morning. Goodnight, my beautiful wife. Sleep well.'

He went down the stairs into the silence, leaving her alone in the moonlight.

Julia opened reluctant eyes the following morning to the sound of hammering. At first she thought it must be some special kind of migraine, brought on by wretchedness and lack of sleep, then she realised it was coming from outside the house.

She got slowly out of bed, looking with loathing at the dress she had worn the day before. There was no way she was putting it on again before it had been laundered.

The word made her wince as she saw the pile of clothes Alex had so cynically discarded the night before.

She averted her gaze and went over to the chest, extracting the other dress. It fitted no better than the first one had done, but she supposed she should be thankful that Alex allowed her the privilege of a change of clothing at all.

She put on her sandals and went carefully down

the wooden stairway and out into the open,
following the sound of the hammering. Alex was
there, fitting what seemed to be a new window-frame
to the aperture at the front of the house.

Julia swallowed. *'Kalimera.'*

He flung her a caustic glance. 'Half the morning is
over. I'll have coffee and eggs for breakfast. And
today Penelope will need milking.'

It was like waking from a nightmare, Julia thought,
as she collected some wood for the stove, then going
to sleep again, and finding yourself back in the
middle of the same bad dream.

It took some time to find where the hens were
nesting, and a couple of them did not take kindly to
having their eggs removed. Julia had two nasty pecks
on the hand before she was able to beat a retreat back
to the house.

Penelope was still grazing peacefully. She looked
placid enough, but goats were an unknown quantity
to Julia. She'd seen cows being milked, of course, at
the Home Farm, but the milking shed there, with its
scrupulous hygiene and very latest machinery, was
light years away from conditions here.

She toyed with the idea of telling Alex that she'd
milked Penelope, but spilled the milk on the way
back to the house, but dismissed it wistfully. If the
goat wasn't milked she would be in pain, and there
was no justification for making the poor creature
suffer, no matter how opposed Julia might be to any
kind of involvement with her.

She beat the eggs, then chopped up some potato,
green peppers, onions and tomato, making a kind of
giant tortilla. When it was done, it was fluffy and

golden, filling the kitchen with a warm, savoury smell. Julia brought it to the table, while Alex was rinsing his hands at the sink, and served it out on to two plates. The bread left from the day before was a little stale, but still edible, and she added a chunk to each plate.

Alex sat down and picked up his fork. Julia watched under her lashes, expecting an appreciative look or a brief word of praise for her efforts, but her husband ate every scrap in silence.

When he had finished, she said, 'Did you enjoy that?'

'I was too hungry to notice,' Alex told her curtly. 'Tomorrow you will get up when I do. Apart from your duties, you will have bread to make.'

'I'll have *what*?' Julia dropped the empty plates back on the table with a clatter, searching his face for some leavening gleam of humour, and finding none. She said huskily, 'How much more of this treatment do you think I'm prepared to take?'

'As much as I decide is necessary.' He got to his feet. He was shirtless, and the ancient cream shorts he was wearing clung to his lean hips. 'When you know your place, Julia *mou*, when you've learned to be properly submissive, then I may think again.'

She said very quietly, 'I hate you.'

'Do you, *agapi mou*?' His smile mocked her. 'And yet something tells me I would only have to kiss you—touch you as I did that day by the lake, and you would be drinking from my hand again.' His eyes held her in a challenge as old as the rocky hillside above them. 'Well, shall we put it to the test?'

There was a silence, then Julia shook her head, her

copper hair falling defeatedly across her face. Today, it seemed, she was the vulnerable one.

It irked her all the time she was clearing away the breakfast things, and laboriously heating the water to wash the clothes, to realise how disappointed she had been over his failure to praise her cooking. Yet he was quick enough to criticise when things went wrong, she thought rebelliously.

It took her an hour to wash the clothes. She had never realised before how completely she had taken for granted the automatic washing machine and tumble-dryer at Ambermere. Not that she'd used them very often, she reminded herself ruefully. Mrs Parsons emptied the linen baskets and did the laundry, and a woman from the village came in to do the ironing. And a lot of the sweaters and blouses that she and her mother wore required careful hand washing, she recalled, grimacing, as she laboriously tried to wring the excess water out of Alex's jeans.

She put the wet garments in a plastic bowl and carried them outside.

'Is there a washing line?' she asked.

'No.' He had almost finished the window, she noticed. 'Spread the clothes in the sun. They will soon dry.'

Now why didn't I think of that? Julia asked herself wryly. She went to the back of the house and spread the garments carefully over some convenient bushes, watched with disapproval by the hens, and with her usual curiosity by Penelope.

'I suppose I should milk you,' Julia told her conspiratorially. 'But I can't face it yet. What was it the Vicar used to say? Sufficient unto the day is the evil thereof.'

She wandered back to the house, and stood watching Alex as he deftly applied putty to the remaining cracks round the frame.

'Where did you learn to do that?' she asked.

'Here, and in other places.'

'Was that your work before . . .'

'Before I hijacked the Constantis millions?' he supplied drily. 'No, *pedhi mou*. I learned to do it because it needed to be done, and I was the man of the house.'

And Argoli wasn't a society where there were useful workmen at the other end of a phone, or even money to pay them, Julia thought, abashed.

She said, 'Why are you doing it?'

'Because the other frames have rotted. I removed them on a previous visit.'

'No, I didn't mean that. If no one lives here, and there's no chance of them returning for some time, isn't it rather a wasted effort?'

'I do not think so. After all, Julia *mou*, we live here.'

'Yes, but only temporarily.'

He turned, the dark brows lifting sardonically. 'What makes you think so?'

Julia stared at him. 'Well, it's obvious. You're the head of heaven knows how many companies, world-wide. Sooner or later you'll have to go back to the real world.'

'But for me *this* was once the real world,' he said softly. 'Suppose I have decided this is what I prefer? That I am tired of jets and anonymous capital cities that all look the same. Tired of the endless deals and the boardroom wrangles. That I want back the simple life I once knew.' His smile taunted her. 'Maybe even that I want my son to be born here as I was.' He saw the shock in her eyes, and his smile widened. 'That startles you, *ne*? You thought that in spite of everything I would still allow you to have your proud dream—to bear a child for Ambermere, perhaps even give it your name.' He shook his head. 'No, my lovely wife.'

Her lips parted to tell him the thought of Ambermere had not, incredibly, crossed her mind. That it was the prospect, however distant, of carrying his child inside her which had sent her suddenly and dizzily rocking back on her heels.

But that was something she could never admit to him.

She lifted her head, smiling coolly in response. 'So, what's your proud dream, Kyrios Alexandros? To keep me here, barefoot and pregnant?'

He said slowly, 'And if so, what will you do? Plead for mercy?'

Julia shook her head. 'It won't be necessary.' The dark eyes narrowed in challenge, but she carried bravely on. 'You're your father's son, and you can't just—turn your back on your responsibilities. Besides, you've tasted power now and you like it. Bringing me here, making me jump through all these hoops, is just an example. You've done it, because you can. You couldn't revert to being Alex Nobody again, even if you wanted to. And I don't believe you really want to.'

'How confidently you speak,' he said silkily. 'Yet how little you really know me. Must I remind you, *agapi mou*, that you are still a stranger to my heart, and to my bed?'

Julia shrugged. 'For the moment,' she said, keeping her tone almost nonchalant. 'But that won't last for ever—not if you want the son you've been talking about.'

'I want a child.' The last lingering trace of amusement had disappeared from his face. 'What I have yet to decide, Julia *mou*, is if I wish you to be his mother.'

Pain slashed at her as if he had lifted his hand and struck her down. She gave a small inarticulate cry and ran from him, her sandals slipping on the rough stones, down the street between the empty houses, towards the sea.

CHAPTER SEVEN

JULIA sat on the edge of the crumbling breakwater, her back against the remains of a concrete post, gazing unseeingly at the point where sea and sky merged in a haze of exquisite blue.

It didn't seem possible that she could hurt so much, and still go on living.

She could have borne anything rather than the knowledge that Alex did not consider her fit to have his baby. It was after all the ultimate degradation, especially when, barely minutes before, her body had reacted joyously and spontaneously, filling with trembling warmth, at the mere idea of conceiving his child and carrying it under her heart.

I should have known, she thought, her throat constricting in agony. I should have known.

She had asked herself how they could ever have a real relationship after the way their marriage had begun. Well, now she knew. Alex had no intention of keeping her as his wife.

She closed her eyes, damming back the tears that threatened to overwhelm her. What good would crying do?, She had to look ahead, try and make some kind of plan for when he tired of his cruel game he was playing with her, and let her go. And soon she would, but not now. All her tired brain could come up with now was images of Alex—the dismissal in his eyes, the sneer in his voice.

She pulled herself to her feet, brushing the dust from her crumpled dress, and began to wander along the breakwater, trying to imagine the tiny harbour as it must have been in its heyday with dark-sailed caiques tied up along the quay, and groups of fishermen mending their chats, and talking with that peculiar Mediterranean intensity which suggests that World War Three may be declared at any minute.

She tried to smile at her own picture, but it blurred, and she stood for a while, head bent, fighting to regain her composure.

When at last she lifted her head again, the boat was there, crossing the mouth of the harbour—a sharp-lined sailing dinghy, with a single occupant, its blue sails making the most of the afternoon breeze.

For a moment Julia stared at it as if she'd seen an apparition. There might be no one else on Argoli, she thought dazedly, but there could well be other inhabited islands close by. Islands with airports, or even ferry services back to Piraeus. She hadn't looked, she hadn't explored. She'd barely moved outside a fifty-yard radius of the house since she had arrived.

The boat was travelling briskly towards the rocky promontory which formed the other side of the harbour.

Julia began to run frantically along the breakwater, waving her arms in the air.

'Ahoy there!' she shouted. 'Oh, stop—come back, please!'

For one heart-stopping moment she thought the solitary sailor had seen her, that his head had turned towards her where she stood at the very end of the breakwater, dancing in frustration. It was all the encouragement she needed. She kicked off her sandals and dived into the sea.

It was colder than she'd bargained for, and she came up gasping, only to see the dinghy passing swiftly and unheedingly beyond the promontory, and out of sight.

'Oh, no!' Julia managed through chattering teeth, before she began to swim swiftly and desperately after it. She had covered a couple of hundred yards before she realised that she was being utterly ridiculous. That she hadn't a hope in hell of catching up with the dinghy, even if the man in it really had seen her—of which there wasn't the slightest guarantee.

She was nearer the rocks of the promontory now than she was the breakwater, so she began to swim slowly and despondently towards them, letting the buoyancy of the water lift her, barely moving her arms and legs.

The splash she heard barely registered until, with startling suddenness, Alex was beside her in the water, his hands reaching for her with a strength that would not be denied.

Alarmed, Julia kicked out. 'Let go of me!' she choked through a mouthful of salt water.

'Relax.' His voice was a snarl. 'Stop struggling, you little fool!'

He turned her on to her back, still fighting and gasping, and began to tow her towards the promontory. At its edge was an enormous rock, weathered flat to form a platform rising out of the sea, and it was this Julia found herself being hauled on to, not gently.

She lay there for a minute, coughing up the water she'd swallowed, wiping her streaming eyes. Alex was kneeling a couple of feet away from her, his bronzed chest heaving as he sought to recover his breath.

'*Christos*, Julia,' he said at last, his voice uneven. 'Never do—never contemplate such a thing again!'

He must have seen the boat, she thought, horrified, and guessed her intention to swim to it.

She lifted herself into a sitting position, pushing back her sopping hair with a defiant hand.

'I felt like a swim. I didn't realise it was forbidden.'

'A swim?' he echoed in scornful disbelief. 'In your dress?'

Julia shrugged. 'Why not? The choice of beachwear in this hellhole is strictly limited.'

He said hoarsely, 'Don't lie. When I got down to the beach, you were making no attempt to swim. You were already sinking when I reached you . . .' He closed his eyes with a visible shudder.

Realisation dawned on Julia. 'You thought I was drowning?' she asked. 'You thought I'd thrown myself in—deliberately?' She threw back her head and laughed harshly. 'Overcome by your sadistic treatment of me, no doubt.' She invested her voice with as much scorn as his own. 'Well, you flatter yourself, *kyrie*. Nothing you can say or do would drive me to those lengths, so I'm afraid you had your ducking all for nothing. As I said, I wanted a swim, and I took one. I'm sure the slaves' trade union would allow it.'

She got to her feet, climbed from the platform, and made her way across the narrow stretch of coarse sand to the place where she had left her sandals.

Let him think she'd thrown herself in, she thought almost feverishly as she pushed her damp feet into the unyielding plastic. Let him think anything, as long as he didn't guess about the boat—realise that help could be at hand. She would come down here every day from now on, on the pretext of going for a swim. If one boat had come along, there would have to be others.

Her wet dress felt revoltingly cold and clammy, and she pulled the clinging fabric away from her body with a grimace, wondering if the one she had washed earlier would be dry by now.

Alex was waiting for her. As they walked back up the village street side by side, she was aware of his sideways measuring glance.

He said, 'Julia, you must understand I was concerned when you ran away like that—when you did not come back . . .'

'Oh, I'm sure you were.' She hunched a shoulder. 'What other little menial task did you have lined up for me, I wonder?'

'It wasn't like that.' There was an odd urgency in his voice. 'What I said to you . . .'

'Was no worse than anything else you've said and done since our so-called marriage,' Julia cut in crisply. 'Perhaps I was down at the harbour a long time, but I needed to think—and I have.' She took a breath. 'This—everything about our relationship—has been a grotesque mistake. You don't want me as a wife, and I don't want to go on with this—

farce any longer than I have to. Until you decide to let me go, I'll work for you—not as your wife, but as a servant. The wages I require are my clothes back, and a one-way ticket back to England, and those aren't negotiable.'

'And how precisely do you intend to enforce your demands?'

'I shall go on strike,' she informed him, head high. 'And a hunger strike too. I think you'd have some explaining to do, Kyrios Alexandros, if you allowed your bride to starve to death in front of you!'

There was a silence. Julia waited, wondering frantically what she would do if Alex called her bluff, but at last he shrugged.

'So be it,' he said, without particular emotion. 'My servant, and on those terms.'

She waited for relief to flood through her, but all she felt was a peculiar stultifying numbness.

They arrived back at the house in silence. Alex walked to the chest beside his bed, withdrew a pair of cotton slacks and a towel, then without sparing Julia even a glance, stripped off his wet shorts.

He began to towel himself briskly. Julia stood as if transfixed, her body suffused by that old treacherous heated yearning as she watched him.

He said almost casually, still not looking at her, 'A servant should not be in the room when her master is naked. Go and occupy yourself elsewhere.'

Pressing her hands to her burning face, Julia fled back into the sunshine.

Stumbling a little, she made her way round to the back of the house, and stopped with a cry of horrified incredulity. Penelope turned and gave her a look of mild enquiry, the remains of the red dress hanging from the corner of her mouth.

'Oh, God!' Julia wailed. She grabbed the dangling fabric and pulled at it frantically. For a moment the goat resisted, her jaws still working rhythmically, then she released the material, and Julia sat down heavily, what was left of her dress clamped to her breast. 'You bloody animal,' she yelled. 'Just because I wouldn't milk you!'

'What's the matter?' Alex spoke from just behind her.

'This.' Breast heaving, eyes sparking, Julia scrambled to her feet, holding out the well-chewed remnants.

Alex surveyed them with raised brows, as he fastened the waistband of his pants. 'Goats will eat anything. Didn't you know that.'

'No, I didn't!' she raged. 'I notice she didn't eat any of your bloody things. I suppose you trained her specially!'

A muscle twitched beside Alex's mouth. 'She did not eat my clothes, *pedhi mou*, because she could not reach them. Her tether would not permit it. If you'd put the dress in a different place . . .'

'Oh, of course it's my fault!' Julia felt hysteria rising within her. 'I was supposed to know the rotten little beast has a stomach like a dustbin . . .' As Alex doubled up suddenly, his shoulders shaking, her voice rose. 'Don't you laugh at me you bastard! Don't—you—dare laugh . . .' She launched herself at him, her clenched fists pummelling his chest and shoulders, her nails raking at him.

Even off guard as he undoubtedly was, Alex was

too quick for her, his fingers pinioning her furious hands at the wrist, his other arm circling her, drawing her forward against the cool dampness of his skin.

'That is enough,' he ground out, as she tried to kick his shins. 'Calm yourself.' He shook her slightly.

'Let go of me, damn you!' Almost crying with temper, Julia glared up at him, and caught her breath at the sudden intensity in his dark gaze.

He said huskily, 'Do not give me orders, Julia *mou*, not now, or at any time.'

He bent his head and his mouth came down on hers, parting her lips, invading her mouth with a kind of controlled savagery.

She moaned in her throat and tried to pull free, but his hand tangled in her mass of wet copper hair, enforcing her submission, holding her still while his mouth and tongue tasted her, drank from her, drained her until she trembled in his arms.

The scent of his skin, with its faint lingering tang of salt, seemed all she could breathe. Her hands lifted not to claw but to cling, as the sun dazzled on her closing eyelids, and her soft mouth answered the hunger of his kiss with her own.

His hands swept down her body through the wet cling of the dress, seeking, moulding every line and curve of her slender figure, lingering on her breasts, the gentle swell of her hips, her graceful thighs. She gasped, pressing herself against him, as his caress became suddenly, dizzyingly more intimate. His tongue thrust against hers more fiercely as his hand touched her, stroked, explored and tantalised.

A wordless cry broke from Julia, smothered against

his mouth, but it was enough to shatter the fragile sexual thrall that held them.

Alex tore his mouth from hers with a groan, a dark flush heightening the slash of his cheekbones.

He said something in his own language that was almost a snarl, and pushed her away from him. Julia's legs were like water, and she collapsed down on to the stubble of grass, conscious of nothing but the sensuous, yearning throb of her body which only he could satisfy.

She tried to say his name, hold out her hand to him, but his eyes looked down at her almost blindly, the swift, unsteady rise and fall of his chest revealing his own chaotic emotions.

He said hoarsely, half to himself, 'I did not—intend that.'

He turned and walked away, leaving her there, huddled on the grass, staring after him, her eyes wide with bewilderment, and new hurt.

Julia removed the milk pail to a safe distance and got up, giving Penelope a consoling slap on the flank. 'There you are, you monster,' she whispered.

The first time she had tried milking the goat, Penelope had reacted to her initial struggles by kicking the milk over. The second time, she had kicked Julia quite painfully on the knee. They had now reached a stage of cautious neutrality.

Odd, Julia thought, as she carried the milk back to the house, how you got used to all kinds of things which had once seemed totally impossible. She sniffed the smell of baking bread as she stepped into the dimness of the house, and set the pail down, wiping some beads of sweat from her forehead. The first loaf she had made had been an unmitigated disaster, its shape and texture like a housebrick.

But she had improved since then, out of sheer necessity, and although she would have won no prizes, her bread was at least eatable.

Practice makes perfect, she thought wryly. She had collected some water from the spring earlier, and now she filled a glass and stood in the doorway sipping it gratefully, and looking up at the shimmer of the sun on the high rocks.

A week had passed, but she still hadn't been able to put those shattering moments in Alex's arms out of her mind, try as she might.

Alex had not returned to the house until late that evening, his face shuttered and forbidding, and Julia had not dared asked where he'd been. Nor had she found the courage to refer to what had transpired in those stolen, sun-drenched minutes, and Alex had never indicated by either word or gesture that he even remembered the incident had taken place. Julia supposed she should be grateful for that.

She told herself so often. But her body, aroused for a fulfilment it had been so harshly denied, was unconvinced.

She drove herself hard, getting up while the sun was still low in the sky, and doing the chores, which had once seemed so difficult, and were now a matter of routine. It was good to get the bulk of the work over before the real heat of the day, she'd discovered. And it also meant she had more time to herself.

She used it to explore every inch of the island. The interior was rocky and barren, but its very starkness had a beauty all its own, she found. And on the other side of the island there were a couple of small but spectacular beaches with firm golden sand shelving gently into the warm and lazy sea.

Julia had wondered to begin with why the village hadn't sprung up around them, the island's most obvious amenity, then castigated herself for thinking like a tourist. A fishing community needed a harbour with sufficient draught for its boats, not a beach to sun itself on.

She had also found where the dinghy had come from, or thought she had. There was another island lying to the west, and much bigger than Argoli, a humped shape, with mountains on the horizon.

But although she had kept her eyes skinned, she had seen no more blue sails, or any other colour, for that matter.

Her explorations also gave her an excellent excuse for avoiding Alex. Since that day in the garden he had treated her, as she had requested, like a servant. There were no more taunting jibes to skin her raw, but those, she thought, she would almost prefer to the icy formality with which he now treated her. The only time she was in his company for any length of time was during meals, and she was aware all the time they were together of a sharp tension between them, dangerous as an electric current.

During the day he was as busy as she was, working on the repairs to the house, which was beginning to look quite prosperous, especially as it had received another coat of whitewash. It was in the evening, when the light faded and the moon rose, that the walls seemed to close in on them, reminding them that they were alone together.

Julia had formed the habit of slipping away to her room as soon as the velvet darkness began to encroach. It was impossible to sit in a room with someone and not speak or even look at him.

But looking held danger. When she was sure he was unaware, she would study him under her lashes almost obsessively, committing him, face and body, to memory against the day when she would never see him again.

It was madness, and she knew it. The sensible thing would be to start erasing him from her mind, so that she could ultimately pretend these burning, tormenting days had never happened.

Each night she lay awake, watching the moon until it faded, and she could fall at last into an uneasy sleep. But even there she wasn't safe. Her dreams were torture, where he held her, caressing her, murmuring love words to her, yet always without the ultimate possession, so that she woke, perspiring and feverish, her body clamouring for satisfaction, her arms reaching for him.

Most days Alex went fishing, and Julia seized the opportunity to wash the hated green dress, wrapping herself sarong-style in a towel while she did so. Then she would go down to the harbour, and the stone platform by the sea, or one of the beaches, spread the dress out, and swim or sunbathe in the nude until it was dry.

She had to reluctantly admit that she had probably never looked better, apart from the shadows under her eyes induced by her disturbed nights. But whereas most brides had good reason to look like that, she thought unhappily, she had none. She had always been slim, but now she was lithe, her muscles taut with the unaccustomed exercise she had been taking. Her skin was golden too, without a strap mark or a bikini line to spoil the perfection of her tan.

What a waste! she thought wryly.

She glanced down at herself and pulled a face. The green dress had never been vibrant, but its constant immersions and bleachings had faded it badly. And she was aware she had been in contact with Penelope too.

Laundry time again, she thought with a sigh. Sometime later, the dress in a wet bundle under her arm, she made her way unhurriedly to her favourite beach, about half a mile from the village. Here two leaning rocks had formed a slight hollow filled with pale gold sand, and an olive tree at the edge of the beach provided some welcome shade in the hottest midday hours.

She spread the dress on a rock, dropped the towel on the sand, and ran to the sea.

It was at times like this that she could almost be happy, she thought, as she turned and twisted like a mermaid in the water. She could forget that her marriage was a disaster, a failure as soon as it had begun. She could nearly, but not quite, forget the man who had awoken her to passion's possibilities, without teaching her its consummation. She wondered whether there would ever be sufficient time or circumstance to wipe Alex from her mind and emotions, or whether she would be left scarred for ever.

Sighing, she stood up and began to wade back

towards the shore, wringing the water out of her hair as she did so, lifting her face to the warmth of the sun.

As she stepped through the shallows on to the sand, she saw him. He was standing like a statue beside the rock where her dress hung. His face was unsmiling, almost ravaged as he watched her walking towards him.

Julia stopped. She had nothing to cover herself with. Alex was standing between her and the towel. She could always, she supposed in some distant corner of her mind, hide herself with her hands.

Although he was so still, she could see a muscle working in his throat—could see the flagrant starvation in his eyes as he looked at her.

He said, wearily, as if he had returned from a long journey, *'Ti orea pou ise.* How beautiful you are!'

She lifted her hands almost languidly and swept the mass of damp curling hair back from her shoulders. She was Eve. She was all woman, and she smiled at him. Then, without haste, she began once more to walk towards him.

By the time she reached him he was naked too, his clothes almost wrenched from him. His arms closed round her, and their mouths and bodies met. He stormed her with kisses, her lips exploring her face and throat with frantic need. They sank together to the warm sand behind the wall of rock, their clothes making a bed for them.

Julia had dreamed Alex would kiss her like this, caressing the hollows in her throat, finding her pulse points and setting them throbbing like jungle drums. She had longed to feel the tenderness of his hands on her breasts, fondling the soft curves, stroking the rosy nipples with his fingers and tongue until they stood proudly erect. The reality was a delight that was almost pain.

His lips moved downwards on an erotic journey over each sun-gilded contour, whispering his pleasure, his desire against her skin. Half afraid, Julia began to touch him in turn, her hands shaping his shoulders, and the long strength of his back, down to the taut buttocks.

She hesitated, and Alex kissed her mouth and carried her hands to his body, showing her without words what he wanted. She was shy at first, wary of his sheer male power, but he murmured husky-throated encouragement as her fingers became more assured, and then more wanton, making him groan softly.

Alex bent his head and laid a trail of light, teasing kisses across her flat stomach, and down to the joining of her thighs. She was melting, longing for his touch, but the first intimate, sensuous brush of his lips shocked her into sudden tension. Her hands tugged at his hair.

'No—please . . .'

Alex lifted his head, his dark eyes intent as he laid a silencing finger on her trembling lips.

'Trust me,' he whispered. 'There are many paths to pleasure, my innocent. This is only one of them.'

He bent to her again, and with a little sob Julia abandoned herself to his dictate. Urgency was unfurling deep within her like the petals of some strong, wild flower, running like fire through her veins. Her body began to twist restlessly, her hands clenching and unclenching, her voice whimpering something that might have been his name.

Just as she felt she could bear no more, the need inside her threatening to shatter her into a thousand tiny pieces, Alex moved, suddenly and swiftly, his body covering hers, his hands sliding under her slim hips to lift her towards him.

For one burning moment she felt his warmth and hardness against her, then slowly, and with infinite care, he entered her. For a moment there was pain, and she flinched. Then, feeling him hesitate, terrified that he might draw back, she arched against him, acting out of pure instinct, her hands clinging to his sun-warmed shoulders, her slender legs locking round his waist, knowing triumphantly that the last fragile barrier had been swept aside, and that, at last, he was totally sheathed inside her.

For a brief while they remained still, Alex's face almost tortured as he looked at her.

He said unsteadily, 'I have wanted this—so much, you cannot know . . .'

'Can't I?' Her voice broke as, slowly and sweetly, he began to move on her, inside her, with her. 'Oh, Alex—*Alex* . . .'

She felt the rhythm he had initiated, joined it, let it possess her, marvelling, as she did so, at its tenderness, its simplicity. They kissed, gently at first, lips and tongues searching out each other's secrets with a growing wonderment, then with a fierce sensual passion which reflected the deepening thrusts of their seeking bodies.

The first slow convulsion of sensation inside her took Julia almost unaware. The next made her cry out in mingled joy and pain, as the pleasure took her, carried her mindlessly to some other dimension of time and space, held there suspended in a sweet agony which threatened to tear her apart. She felt Alex shudder wildly in her arms, his voice groaning something in his own language as he reached his climax in turn.

Slowly, still wrapped, enfolded in each other, they drifted back to reality. Julia felt languid, boneless with voluptuous contentment. As Alex began to move away from her, she halted him, twining her arms round his neck, sliding her hands over his sweat-slicked shoulders.

'Don't leave me,' she whispered, huskily, her eyes shining with invitation and promise. 'Not yet . . .'

But there was no answering smile in the dark gaze that surveyed her. Almost casually, he reached up and detached her clinging hands, freeing himself totally from her embrace. He rolled away from her and lay, trying to control his unsteady breathing, an arm flung across his face.

Julia propped herself up on one elbow, uncertainty settling like a stone inside her, as she watched him.

'Alex?' She put out a hand and touched his face timidly. 'Is something wrong?'

'What could be wrong?' Alex sat up and reached for his jeans. 'You were as warm and willing as any man could wish. I hope you were equally satisfied?'

Colour rushed into Julia's face. 'It was—wonderful.' She tried to speak evenly. 'So—why—why don't you . . .?'

'Have you again?' he cut across her faltering words, with brutal directness, as he fastened his zip.

'Yes.' She made herself meet his gaze.

He laughed harshly, his eyes flicking insolently over her nakedness. 'So eager, *agapi mou?*' he asked. 'So greedy for me? Or do you just wish to boast to that woman in England about your—Greek stud?' He smiled without amusement at the expression of dawning horror in her face. 'I see you understand me at last. So you must also understand why I must disappoint you.'

He rose to his feet. 'Enjoy your memories, my beautiful wife. They are all that you will have,' he added with icy quietness, and walked away from her.

CHAPTER EIGHT

JULIA stumbled back to the village, looking neither to right nor left, oblivious to everything but the pain of this final blow.

She could remember in searing detail every taunt, every snide innuendo that Tricia Bosworth had uttered, and the total recall made her blood run cold.

But she had put the whole distasteful incident out of her mind, she thought desperately. She hadn't mentioned Mrs Bosworth's visit to her room to a soul. So how—how had Alex known? Had Mrs Bosworth sought him out—made some kind of insinuation? It didn't seem possible, even for her.

By the time she had struggled back into her dress and sandals, and gone after him to try and explain, Alex had been out of sight, and although she had run to the top of the track which led down to the beach, calling his name, there had been no reply.

But when she did catch up with him, would he believe the truth—that she had been shocked and digusted by Tricia Bosworth's remarks, but had written them off as another example of her malice? It did not seem altogether likely.

Her stance might have had more credibility if she hadn't called him a peasant—and said all those other things to his face, she thought wretchedly.

In her distress, she missed the path she usually took, and finally emerged at the side of the harbour scrambling, uncaring of bruised toes and grazed arms and legs, over the rocks of the promontory

The sailing dinghy, its blue sail neatly furled, was moored beside the breakwater.

Julia stood motionless, staring across at it, her heart thudding.

There was no one around. All she had to do was climb aboard and sail away. She had handled boats like it a dozen times. And it wasn't like stealing, she appeased her conscience feverishly. When she reached the big island she would make some explanation to the authorities—ensure the lone mariner was rescued.

She had to get away from Argoli—away from Alex who hated her, who only wanted to punish her, who had even made love to her out of some kind of perverted revenge.

Well, she couldn't take any more. She'd had enough of his cruelty—his neglect. He had shown her paradise, then condemned her to a lonely hell. Let him stay in it alone, she thought, swallowing the painful lump in her throat.

Keeping a wary eye open for the returning owner, Julia trod round to the breakwater. The dinghy was quite new, and clearly very expensive. She cast a practised eye over the equipment. It was ideally designed for single-handed use.

So what was she waiting for? All she had to do was climb down into the thing. She could feel the faint breeze stealing across the water, beckoning her to freedom . . .

She shivered suddenly, wrapping her arms round her body. Freedom, she thought bitterly. What freedom was there without Alex? Separation from him would be a prison, with eternal solitary confinement.

She went on staring down almost compulsively at the boat, aware of a deep and terrible trembling spreading through her body.

The means of her release had come far too late, she thought dazedly. Standing there, more alone than she had ever been in her life, she realised suddenly and completely that she loved Alex—that she had probably been in love with him almost from the first. That was why she had agreed to that whirlwind marriage, she thought, her nails digging into the palms of her hands. Not for Ambermere, but because she wanted to be with him always. She had fooled herself with reasons, with rational arguments, but in truth, it was as simple as that.

It's taken all this time for me to understand, she thought wonderingly. If we'd had a normal marriage—the usual honeymoon, I'd probably have admitted it long ago, but Argoli—this whole mess got in the way. And Ambermere, beloved though it is, has been just another obstacle, preventing me from seeing how I really felt—what I really wanted.

And if our marriage had been a conventional one, perhaps I still wouldn't have faced up to the truth. Maybe I'd still be telling myself that I'd sacrificed myself for Ambermere. Alex brought me to Argoli to teach me a lesson—and I've learned to know myself at last, but too late.

The sad finality of the words in her head made her shiver.

But I can't leave him, she told herself desperately. I'll never leave while there's even a remote chance I can win him over, make him change his mind about me. He wanted me today, and that's a beginning. I can make him want me again, somehow, she thought with a pang of nostalgia for all the lovely seductive clothes, the cosmetics and the scent, aboard the *Clio* and long gone, looking down with a grimace at the tatty green dress, her broken fingernails and callused hands.

And if desire is all there is, if I can never make him care for me in the way I need—then I'll live with that somehow.

This is what he's brought me to—yearning for a smile from him, a kind word. And, God help me, I wouldn't have it any other way.

She turned slowly, away from the boat, and walked up the street to the house.

A man was emerging from the front door, hands thrust into the pockets of immaculate white shorts. His blue and white shirt was open to the waist, and his swarthy face wore a brooding frown.

The lone sailor had been exploring, Julia thought—then stopped with a faint gasp as she realised who he was.

She wanted to turn and run into one of the empty houses, and hide, but it was too late. He had seen her, and lengthened his stride.

Julia stood her ground, moistening dry lips with the tip of her tongue as she saw the total incredulity in his face.

'Julia?' he asked uncertainly. 'Julia Kendrick? But this is not possible!'

Julia gave him a neutral smile. 'Hello, Paul. How are you?'

Paul Constantis went on staring at her, his brows drawn together in a frown of disbelief. 'I think I am going out of my mind! Argoli has been deserted for years, No one ever comes here.'

Julia shrugged. 'Yet here I am, she countered, trying to speak lightly, as her mind ran in circles trying to think what to say—what to do.

He said slowly, 'Then it was you I saw that day.' He gave a strained laugh. 'I thought it was a hallucination. A girl with red hair waving at me from an empty place—a desolation.' He spoke the words with distaste, his eyes narrowing as he looked at her, really seeing her for the first time. 'But what are you doing here—what has happened to you, in the name of God? Were you shipwrecked—has there been some disaster?'

He was comparing her present appearance with that of the chic and soignée girl he had taken to dinner some lifetime ago, she realised.

She said, carefully, 'Not exactly. It—it's difficult to explain . . .'

'No,' Alex said, coldly and quietly, 'it is perfectly simple.'

Neither of them had heard him approach, yet there he was, standing only a few yards from them. Julia jumped, and Paul Constantis swung round as if he had been electrocuted.

'Alexandros?' The word emerged as a croak.

'You?'

Alex shrugged. 'Why not?' He stared at Julia, his face icily cynical. 'Well, *pedhi mou*—tell my cousin Paul how you came here, and why. He is waiting to hear, and I am sure he will find the story quite—fascinating.'

Paul Constantis's eyes went from one to the other, his face sharpening into sudden avidity. He attempted a laugh. 'Is there some mystery? I—I did not know you two were even acquainted. I am clearly intruding . . .'

Julia lifted her chin. 'Yes, you are, rather,' she said, smiling to rob the words of offence. 'You see, Alex and I are here on our honeymoon.'

There was a moment of intense silence, then Paul Constantis began to laugh.

'This is a joke, *ne*? It is only a few weeks since we parted, Julia *mou*, and you claim in that time to have met my cousin Alexandros—to have married him? It is impossible!'

'But it's also the truth.' Julia wasn't sure her legs would obey her, but she forced them into action to cross the distance that separated her from Alex, so that she could stand beside him. He made no welcoming gesture, but he didn't turn away either. 'Alex and I have been married for—nearly ten days, haven't we, darling?'

His face was guarded. 'Yes.'

'But it cannot have happened! There would have been some news—some announcement—the papers would have picked up such a marriage.' Paul Constantis wasn't laughing any more. He dragged a handkerchief out of his pocket and wiped his forehead. 'Why wasn't the family told?'

'I told my mother,' Alex said drily. 'I imagined she would have—broken the news. As you are here now, I presume you are staying with her.'

'Yes, all of us,' Paul said thickly. 'She invited us—said it was time for a reconciliation, that she had a surprise for us. We thought'—he stopped suddenly —'that is, we did not imagine . . .'

'I understand,' Alex's voice deepened ironically. 'And now you know.'

'Yes,' said Paul, almost biting out the words. 'Now I know.' He looked them both over, frowning. 'But what are you doing here? A honeymoon in this place, *po po po.* No man would do such a thing to his bride. No woman could accept it . . .'

'Haven't you ever heard of a working honeymoon?' Julia broke in calmly, her heart thumping. 'All the usual places seemed so—boring and conventional. When Alex mentioned that he was thinking of restoring this house on a deserted island, it sounded quite incredibly romantic.' She slid her hand into Alex's unresponsive clasp. 'And it's been wonderful, hasn't it, darling? We've done such a lot of work on the house. It will make a marvellous retreat when it's finished—somewhere quiet to bring our children . . .'

'Ah, yes,' Paul said meditatively. His glance touched the unbecoming folds of the green dress at Julia's waist, slid down and away. 'Now perhaps I understand—this hasty marriage.'

There was another silence, and Julia felt a wave of heat sweep over her as she realised what Paul was getting at. Her lips parted in angry protest, then closed as Alex pressed her fingers warningly.

'But you are right that it is quiet here. In fact it is almost—primitive.' Paul's good-looking face wore an overt sneer, and Julia remembered, with an inward wince, that she had caught him emerging from the house. 'You are very brave, Julia *mou*, and very loyal to endure such conditions.'

'There's not much endurance called for,' Julia returned crisply. 'Alex is my husband, and wherever he goes, that's where I want to be.'

'What a charming sentiment!' Paul turned to Alex. 'No wonder you kept your marriage so secret, my cousin! Any man would wish to enjoy such love—such devotion in uninterrupted bliss.' He shook his head in mock regret. 'And then I had to blunder in! But when I saw Julia in the distance at the harbour some days ago, I had the strangest impression that she was in distress—that she needed help. Isn't that absurd?'

'Quite absurd.' Julia rested her head against Alex's rigid shoulder. 'Especially when you only caught a glimpse—and even then you thought I was a hallucination.'

'And instead you are Alex's bride, and only too real,' Paul Constantis said, his smile humourless. 'So—when do you plan to leave this—idyllic seclusion?'

'Now that our secret has been discovered, there is small point in remaining,' Alex replied brusquely. 'When you return to Lymnos, please ask my mother to send Yannis for us at once.'

'With the greatest of pleasure.' The charming

mask was back in place. 'Does she know you are
here?'

'No. She understands that a honeymoon is a
private affair.'

'Of course,' Paul agreed. 'And she is—so good at
respecting secrets, is she not? It will be a wonderful
surprise for her—and also for my family.' His eyes
flicked towards Julia. 'They will enjoy meeting your
new wife, my mother—and my sister Zoe.'

He nodded affably, then walked away towards the
harbour, not looking back. As soon as he was out
of sight, Julia felt Alex move abruptly away from
her.

She said, 'Are we really—leaving here?'

'You heard me say so.' His voice was forbidding.

She swallowed. 'And do I have to meet your
mother—the rest of your family—looking like this?'
She bit her lip. 'Or is it part of the ongoing humbling
process?'

He said roughly, 'Of course not. *Christos*, what do
you take me for? There are clothes for you here, and
have been since the beginning.'

'Then if I might have them, please.' Julia took a
step towards the dark doorway, but Alex halted her,
his hand on her arm.

He said, 'Why did you do that? Why did you
pretend? You could have told him the truth—repaid
me a hundredfold for everything I've made you
suffer here.' He laughed harshly. 'He would have
loved to hear how I've kept you here against your
will—humiliated you in every possible way. He could
have rescued you—carried you off to tell the story of

your wrongs to the world's press. They would have found it a—sensation.' He paused, the dark eyes boring into her face. 'So—why didn't you tell him the truth?'

Because I love you, her heart cried silently. Because my instinct is to protect you, in spite of everything.

She gave him a steady look. 'Perhaps I feel that whatever's happened here is our own private business.' She freed herself gently from his clasp. 'And maybe my thirst for revenge isn't the equal of yours,' she added quietly, and walked into the house, leaving him staring after her.

The loaf of bread she'd made that morning was still in the middle of the kitchen table. She touched its crisp crust with the tip of her finger. Well, that was one accomplishment she would not need again, she thought without any particular pleasure.

She had heard that long-term prisoners sometimes grew to love their jails, and she could believe it, although her stay on Argoli had not been a lengthy one. She seemed to have lost track of time, as one day succeeded the next. But the day that matters—the one I shall remember—is this one, she thought. The day when, however briefly, I belonged to Alex at last.

Her body shivered in delight at the memory of it, then tensed at he walked into the house carrying a suitcase which she recognised as part of the luggage which had accompanied her on to *Clio*.

'You had better change,' he told her brusquely. 'Once Paul delivers my message, the boat will be sent for us at once.'

Julia stared down at the table. 'Won't your mother think this is all rather—strange?'

'Perhaps,' he said, shrugging. 'But she will say little. Her own life has not been lived on particularly conventional lines.'

Julia bit her lip. 'I suppose not,' she said colourlessly. 'Does—does she speak English?'

He gave her a cynical look. 'Afraid of finding yourself in the company of yet another ignorant peasant, Julia *mou?'*

'No.' She shook her head. 'Alex, for God's sake, can't we forget all that nonsense—please? I've paid for the things I said—for the things I thought. Please don't blame me for all that Tricia Bosworth said. I've no idea why she talked in the way she did. She made me feel sick . . .'

'And me too,' he said reflectively. 'That day of our wedding, I was prepared to forget the past. You looked so lovely, so innocent as you came to me, that any thought of punishing you, of salving my pride at your expense, seemed disgusting—grotesque. So I decided to abandon my plan to bring you here. Instead, I thought I would woo you gently to accept me, and the life we would make together. I even wondered if I could make you fall in love with me a little.'

'But Alex . . .'

He held up his hand, silencing her. 'No, listen to me. All that time at the house, surrounded by other people, I was in torture. I wanted so much to be alone with you—to have you to myself. When you went to your room, it seemed to me that you had been gone for ever, so eventually I followed. The door was open—and I—heard everything.'

A smile twisted his lips. 'Oh, I knew why you were marrying me, Julia *mou*. I should have been under no illusion—but, foolishly, I had hoped that you might have begun to regard me differently. And because I knew I'd been a fool, I became angry all over again. so we came here.'

'But you don't think I agreed with all those revolting things she said—those ghastly, twisted lies?' Julia jumped to her feet. 'You can't think that!'

He said harshly, 'I know what I heard, my beautiful wife. And there was not one word of contradiction, of denial from you. You—went along with everything she said.'

'It may have seemed like that,' Julia said desperately. 'But it wasn't. Oh, Alex, you have to believe me! I didn't argue with her because I didn't think she was worth it—didn't want to give her the satisfaction of a scene, or letting her see that she could upset me. I—just wanted her to go. She's a liar—a malicious troublemaker. Anyone would tell you that.'

He said unsmilingly, 'And yet at our first encounter, when she talked of you marrying for Ambermere, she spoke no more than the truth.'

'No,' Julia denied, almost wringing her hands. 'Oh, Alex, you're so wrong . . .'

'Yes,' he said quietly. 'Wrong from the beginning. Wrong about everything.' He shrugged. 'But what does that matter, after all? In these days, a mistake, however grave, does not have to become a lifelong tragedy. We do not have to punish each other any longer. You shall have Ambermere, Julia *mou*, as part of our divorce settlement.'

'You're going to divorce me?' She felt stifled, as if the walls were closing in on her.

'It will be a mutual arrangement, and I hope a civilised one.' His mouth twisted. 'Perhaps our marriage can end in dignity, if nothing else.'

'But it's hardly begun . . .' Julia moistened dry lips with the tip of her tongue. She asked flatly, 'Don't you—want me any more? You—you seemed to . . .'

'My self-control was undermined, *agapi mou*, by the vision of you emerging from the sea like some exquisite Aphrodite.' His smile did not reach his eyes. 'However, I do not—compound my follies.'

'So how do you intend to present me to your mother, to the rest of your family—as your house-keeper?'

'In public you will be my wife, naturally. In private—my guest.' Alex paused. 'We will keep our visit as short as possible, I think.'

'Yes.' Julia's nails were buried painfully in the palms of her hands. 'That would be best.' She paused, trying to force a smile. 'Your mother will be disappointed. I remember you telling me that she—wanted you to be married.'

Alex shrugged. 'Then I will have to ensure her disappointment is kept to a minimum. Fortunately, I do not have to look far for another bride. A year ago, my Aunt Sophia began dropping hints that I should make reparation to the family for the financial loss my existence has caused them by marrying my cousin

Zoe.'

'How very—convenient, for both of you.' Her stiff mouth would barely frame the words. Jealousy wounded her like a savage claw. It took every atom of will-power she possessed not to go on her knees to him, beg him to give their marriage another chance. 'And how does the bride-to-be feel about it?'

His grin was frankly cynical. 'Amenable—what else? In fact, now that she has seen my money slip away from her once, she may even be gratifyingly eager.'

'Then there's nothing more to be said.' Julia picked up the suitcase. 'Thank you for this, at least.'

'I hope there is everything you need,' Alex said courteously. 'Androula packed it, not myself.'

'Then I'm sure it will be fine.' Oh God, how could she mouth these platitudes when her heart was breaking—her entire world falling apart?

He held out his hand. 'Let me take it upstairs for you.'

'No, thank you. I can manage by myself.'

That was something she would have to get used to, she thought, as she walked, head held high, to the wooden stair. Being—by herself. Alone at Ambermere. Once that had been the summit of her ambitions. But the Julia Kendrick who had planned her life in such splendidly selfish isolation had changed—had gone for ever. And in her place was a girl, heartsore and vulnerable, who had come to know what she wanted from life, now and for ever, only to find it was too late. And that her chance of happiness with the man she loved had been cruelly snatched away.

CHAPTER NINE

YANNIS was a small man, broad-shouldered, grizzled of hair, and blue of chin. He greeted Alex like an old friend, pounding him on the back, and pouring out a flood of exuberant Greek.

The smile he turned on Julia revealed crooked teeth, and also a warmth that almost melted the ice round her heart. He took her hands in both of his, growling something in his own language which she could not understand, but the look of intense admiration which accompanied it needed no translation.

He helped her down into the powerful launch which awaited them with exaggerated care.

As they moved out of the harbour, Julia was careful not to look back. Her control was on a knife-edge, she knew, and she could not break down in front of Alex. He might not desire her any more, she thought fiercely, but she would make damned sure he didn't pity her either, because that would be more than she could bear.

The first thing she had seen when she'd opened the suitcase in the privacy of her room had been her wedding dress, and this was what she was now wearing. She had come downstairs almost fearfully, when Alex had called up to say the boat was coming, wondering what his reaction would be. For a breathless moment he had stared at her, his whole attention arrested, then his mouth had tautened cynically, and he'd turned away.

It was the last bid for his attention she would make, Julia told herself drearily, as the launch, with Alex at the wheel, sped towards Lymnos.

The trip took barely half an hour. Time had stood still on Argoli. Now it was rushing past her like the breeze from the sea, as ephemeral as the wake creaming behind them. Reminding her as if she needed such a reminder, how soon her life with Alex would be over.

As they got near the island Julia could see a cluster of white houses, and other buildings, topped by a church, spilling down to the water's edge round a small harbour, but Alex bypassed this, continuing along the coast.

It was very different from Argoli, Julia realised. Apart from its size, Lymnos was greener, with far more trees. The coastline was rimmed by silvery horsehoes of sand, and the interior was almost mountainous. She wondered whether her stay would be long enough to enable her to see something of the island, then dismissed the idea impatiently. That was, after all, the least of her troubles.

The first and most immediate ordeal would be meeting Alex's mother. She tried to form a mental picture of her, but failed completely. Alex had said so little about her, after all, but from the few hints he had dropped, Julia had gathered that his mother was a woman of character.

I wonder what she'll expect me to call her, she thought nervously. I wish I knew more Greek. I'll have to take lessons . . . And stopped, with a pang, as she realised they would never be needed.

It was nearly evening, and the sun was going down over the sea, spilling a path like flame across the restless surface of the water. She found herself wishing, ludicrously, that she could snatch the wheel, send the launch speeding along that glittering path to the edge of the world, to somewhere she could be alone with Alex—where the rest of the human race would never find them.

But there was no chance of that. Already he was turning the wheel, aiming the launch smoothly towards the shore and the small private landing stage which was begnning to take shape in the distance.

There was someone waiting there for them—a woman, clad in elegant violet silk trousers, and a tunic top in a deep pinky-red, like some exotic fuchsia. Shoulder-length tawny hair, discreetly streaked, framed a face that was vibrantly attractive without being in any way classically beautiful, and her irrepressible smile revealed very white teeth as she advanced to meet them, arms outstretched.

Zoe? Julia asked herself, wincing, then breathed again as she realised the newcomer, at close quarters, was considerably older than first impressions suggested. Her face was also unmistakably familiar, she thought with bewilderment.

'Alexandros *mou!*' The woman's voice was deep and throaty, as she threw her arms round Alex's neck and kissed him warmly. 'Wicked one—deceiving me like this, pretending that you were cruising on *Clio* when all the time you were just across the water!' She hugged him again. 'But I do not blame you. A yacht, even when the crew is as well trained as yours, is too public for a honeymoon.' She turned to Julia, almond-shaped eyes sweeping her candidly. 'So you are my new daughter. Welcome to Lymnos, dear child.'

Julia was aware she was gaping, and closed her mouth hurriedly. *This* was Alex's mother? she asked herself dazedly. This was the supposed peasant girl George Constantis was said to have seduced?

Because now she had heard her voice, she could also put a name to that smiling, distinctive face too.

She found her own voice from somewhere. 'You—you are Maria Xanthe.'

'Why, yes,' the older woman said with amusement. 'You seem surprised.'

'I am,' Julia managed. Her heart was thumping, and her throat was dry.

Maria Xanthe, she thought, her mind reeling. The actress who had taken Hollywood by storm years before—flared across its skies like a meteor, then retired at the height of her fame. The actress whose films still enjoyed a cult following all over the world. Maria Xanthe, incredibly, was Alex's mother.

'You mean Alexandros did not tell you?' Maria Xanthe's brows drew together slightly. She turned to him. 'But why not?'

Alex slid an arm round her waist. 'I wanted you to be a surprise for her, *kougla mou.*' He directed an ironic glance at Julia. 'Also, I wished to save my wife from any—further preconceptions.'

'Well, you have succeeded in the first of your aims,' his mother said with faint tartness, giving him a repressive look. 'The poor little one looks as if she has been poleaxed! Perhaps it is not so much a surprise for her as a terrible shock, hmm?'

'Not in the least.' Julia dragged together the rags of her composure. 'Anyway, I should be used to Alex's—surprises by now. This is a great honour, Madame Xanthe. I've seen all your films.'

The actress laughed. 'No, it is not possible—you are too young. Ah, but there is English television, of course.' She gave Julia a bland look. 'And which of my films did you most enjoy, child?'

Julia realised she was being gently tested. She said, 'Well, *Darkness at Dawn* is the one they show most often, but I prefer *North of the City.*'

Maria Xanthe gave her an approving look. 'It is a favourite of mine too.' She slid her arm through Julia's and began to lead her along the landing stage towards the small beach, and the gardens beyond. 'I am going to like this beautiful girl you have married,' she tossed laughingly over her shoulder to Alex. 'I forgive you for hiding her away from us all on Argoli.' She turned back to Julia. 'It is sad to see the island deserted, *ne?* It was once so busy, so happy—so important to me. Now, I can hardly bear to go there.'

'It will be happy again, Mama,' Alex said quietly. 'When the people return.'

Maria Xanthe laughed. 'When he first said that to me, I thought it was just a dream. But I know now that what my Alexandros says, he does, no matter what the cost to himself or his resources.' She squeezed Julia's arm. 'So be warned, little one.'

'I think I've already discovered that for myself,' Julia said quietly.

'So soon? *Po po po.* But then you have been quite alone, with nothing to do with your days and nights but—find out about each other and about love. That is good, I think.'

Julia smiled weakly in response. Nothing to do, she thought wryly. How little Madame Xanthe knew! Clearly she imagined they had been sharing some sun-baked idyll together.

She wondered how her mother-in-law would react if she told her, 'My days were filled with the hardest manual labour I ever dreamed of, with no time off for good behaviour, and my nights were spent tossing and turning on the grottiest mattress in western civilisation, longing for a lover who never came to me.' Perhaps it would be Maria Xanthe's turn to be poleaxed.

The villa was beautiful, a gracious, rambling structure, hung with bougainvillaea, and all white except for the doors and louvred window shutters, which had been made from some rich, dark wood.

Madame Xanthe nodded when she saw Julia's entranced expression. 'You like my home? It is yours too now.'

Julia began to say something deprecatory and grateful, encountered Alex's harshly cynical glance, and subsided into wretched silence.

Inside, it was exquisitely cool, with large old-fashioned fans whirling on the ceiling.

'They are for show,' said Maria Xanthe, kicking off her high-heeled sandals and walking barefoot across the marble tiles of the wide hall. She gave Julia a conspiratorial grin. 'We have air-conditioning too—something I grew to rely on during my time in

America.' She threw open a massive pair of double doors. 'Now, come and meet the others.'

Julia knew a cowardly impulse to turn and run, then, steeling herself, she followed Maria Xanthe into the room beyond.

It was an awkward little tableau which confronted her. The first person she saw was Paul, clearly on edge, and standing behind a sofa on which two women were seated.

One of them was no longer young, her face lined and haughty. She was wearing the traditional black of a widow, but her dress was made from silk and complemented lavishly with diamonds at wrist and throat.

'Julia, may I present to you Madame Sophia Constantis, who is my guest here. Paul, her son, I believe you already know. And this is Madame's daughter Zoe.'

Zoe Constantis was a beautiful girl, sloe-eyed and olive-skinned, with a sleekly voluptuous body discreetly displayed in an expensive orchid pink dress. Her good looks were currently marred by the sullen expression she made no effort to dissemble. She shook hands with Julia, as did her mother, but their greetings were perfunctory in the extreme, and the looks which accompanied them were positively inimical.

If Alex hadn't already told her Madame Constantis's plans for Zoe and himself, she would have little trouble guessing, Julia thought with irony.

She watched Alex step forward, kiss his aunt's hand and cheek, then turn to Zoe, and looked away abruptly. I—cannot—watch him kiss her, she thought

savagely, feigning an interest in a large portrait of
Maria Xanthe which hung above the empty fireplace.

'Bah, don't look at that! It is a terrible likeness. The
painter was very young, and a little in love with me,
and his hand shook.' Madame Xanthe gurgled with
laughter as she handed Julia a glass. 'Here, *pedhi mou*.
A dry martini—another American legacy.'

Julia swallowed. 'I don't think . . .'

'Ah, yes, you need it,' her mother-in-law said
firmly. 'You are a little pale suddenly. Maybe you are
tired.' She lowered her voice, giving Julia a
mischievous look. 'Would you prefer to have dinner
alone, in your bedroom perhaps with Alex?' She
sighed. 'If I had known you would visit me, I would
not have filled the house with these other guests. But
I meant it for the best. George would have wished me
to be kind to his family, and we cannot always be
enemies.'

'I'm sure Alex agrees with you.' Julia took a sip of
her martini, and gasped. 'Wow!'

'Strong, eh?' Julia was treated to that outrageous
grin again. 'It is what you need, little one. You are
tense, I think. One moment you are alone with my
Alex, making love, the next you are surrounded by
these people who look at you as if you are a bad
smell.' She nudged Julia gently. 'But you are not
alone. How do you think they looked at me when we
first met? They must have asked themselves a
thousand times what kind of woman I would be.' She
giggled softly. 'The truth sent them almost into a
frenzy!'

'But surely they already knew,' Julia protested.
'You're so famous, they must have heard of you.'

'Of Maria Xanthe, yes, but that is my acting name. I am really called Maria Cristoforou, and that was the name that appeared on Alex's birth documents. That was why I was able to preserve my anonymity, until I chose to abandon it.' She rolled her eyes comically. 'Can you imagine, *pedhi mou*, the scandal they could have caused if they had known who I really was during that absurd court case? That I could not endure. But now that they depend on Alex to support them, to maintain their lifestyle, they do not dare say a word.' She shrugged a shoulder. 'And who would care now, anyway?' Sudden tears sparkled in the vivid eyes, and were brushed away. 'My poor George has been dead so many years.' She whirled round, clapping her hands for attention as a uniformed maid appeared in the doorway and stood waiting deferentially. 'It is time for dinner.' She took Julia's hand. 'You will sit next to me, my child.'

Julia remembered little about the meal. She tried to eat some of everything that was placed in front of her, but was never sure whether or not she had succeeded. Maria Xanthe controlled the tensions evident round the table with a flow of light, inconsequential chatter which involved everyone.

But all Julia was really aware of was Alex's eyes, like dark chips of obsidian, watching her above the candle flames. She could sense the anger in him, feel it reaching out to her.

Oh, please, she pleaded silently. It's not my fault if your mother likes me—if she's trying to make me feel at home here.

The meal seemed to last for hours, and then there were the tiny cups of thick sweet coffee to be swallowed, with liqueurs which tasted of tangerine. Eventually it was over, and Julia could ask to be shown her room. Madame Xanthe insisted on escorting her there herself.

It was a large room, plainly but comfortably furnished, the coverlet on the wide bed, and the curtains, handwoven in what Madame Xanthe told her was a local design.

'Everything in the house I chose myself,' she said with simple satisfaction. 'I think now you have everything you need—except for your husband, and I will send him to you soon.' She leaned forward and kissed Julia on the forehead, tracing a swift sign of the cross there as well.

'Bless you, little one,' she said. 'Be happy, love my Alex well, and make me a beautiful grandchild.'

She vanished, and Julia was alone. She felt weary to death, but sleep was beyond her. She wandered restlessly round the room, examining everything. She peeped into the small bathroom, staring at the deep tub, the rows of fluffy towels, and the shelves of lotions and essences with a kind of wondering fascination. She had almost forgotten what it was like, she thought, to wallow up to her neck in scented water. Well, she would give herself a practical reminder here and now.

She picked up the nightgown which had been laid out on the bed in readiness, then filled the bath with steaming water, adding a liberal sprinkling of oil, perfumed with carnations. She shampooed her hair and applied conditioner, then lay back, luxuriating in the comfort of the water.

But though her body was relaxed, her mind was

still trapped on the same unhappy treadmill.

If Tricia Bosworth had not come to her room, how different her life would have been! On his own admission, Alex had been having second thoughts about marooning her on Argoli. He had spoken, too, of wooing her gently, she thought with swift pain, and for a moment she indulged herself with a mental image of what that wooing might have been—of herself seduced with warmth and tenderness into passion and its consummation. Then with a little trembling sigh, she wiped it from her mind. It was too poignant to contemplate, and she could torment herself for ever with all these 'might-have-beens'.

She climbed out of the bath and wrapped herself in one of the largest towels, before using the hair-dryer provided. She chose the body lotion that matched the bath oil, rubbing it into her skin, until it was fragrant and glowing, then slipped her nightgown over her head and went back into the bedroom.

Alex was standing by the windows, looking out into the darkness.

He said expressionlessly, without turning his head. 'My mother said you were asking for me.'

Julia flushed. 'No—that is—your mother has a rather romantic view of our relationship,' She swallowed. 'Alex you've got to tell her the truth. It's not fair to let her believe that this a real marriage, She's made me so welcome, I feel a total fraud.'

'Her attitude has created difficulties, certainly,' he said. 'But so has the presence of Thia Sophia and her children. Especially after you played the part of the loyal and loving bride so thoroughly in front of my cousin Paul this afternoon,' he added with faint grimness. 'He will think it curious to say the least if, only a few hours later, we make it known that our marriage is over.' He paused. 'And he may begin to ask the questions we least wish to answer.'

'Yes, I suppose so—but at the time, I couldn't think of anything else to do.' Julia bent her head unhappily. 'What do you suggest?'

'That any public rift should take place after we leave here,' he said curtly. 'It will be easy enough to arrange. My frequent absences on business will provide an undeniable excuse.'

She said tiredly, 'You really have it all worked out, don't you?' She shrugged. 'Well, play it any way you want. But now perhaps you'd leave me alone. I'm rather sleepy.'

He turned slowly and looked at her, the dark eyes sweeping her thinly veiled body in a mocking assessment that made her tingle.

'Leave you, *agapi mou?*' he drawled. 'Now where do you suggest I go?'

'I really don't know,' she shrugged. 'But there must be plenty of other rooms.' She lifted her chin. 'Your cousin Zoe's, for one.

'Ah, yes,' he said softly. 'But my cousin Zoe has her virginity to consider. The first time a man will be allowed into her room, or her bed, will be on her wedding night.'

She said raggedly, 'Then you'll just have to wait, won't you?'

'It seems so.' He paused. 'But while I am waiting, I shall abide by the conventions.' He gave her an edged smile. 'I regret, my wife, that while we remain on Lymnos we shall have to share this room.'

Julia said fiercely, 'No!'

'How fickle you are,' he said derisively. 'Only a few short hours ago, you were clinging to me—begging me, with every inch of your delectable body, to take you again.'

She sank her teeth into her bottom lip, trying to suppress the memories that his contemptuous words had aroused.

'That was then,' she said. 'This is now.'

'Yes,' he said slowly, 'this is now . . .'

He walked towards her, and Julia backed away.

She said on a little breathless note, 'Don't come near me!'

'Is that an order?' mocked Alex.

'It's an appeal to your sense of decency. Our marriage is over, so why—torture me like this?'

'Torture?' he repeated, his brows lifting. 'I heard no screams for mercy earlier.' He put out a hand and slid one of the straps of her nightgown off her shoulder, his thumb stroking her skin.

The breath caught in her throat. 'No—please!'

His fingers lifted to her hair, gently parting the strands that curled on to her shoulders, cupping the slender nape of her neck. She shivered almost convulsively, and Alex stared down at the sudden thrust of her breasts against the apricot silk of the nightgown, his dark eyes kindling, his firm mouth suddenly compressed.

He tugged down the other strap, freeing her from the tiny lace-trimmed bodice. He released its sole fastening, and the silk drifted down to her hips, clung for a second, then whispered to the floor.

He said very quietly, 'No?'

Silence surrounded her, crushed her. She tried to speak, but the muscles of her throat betrayed her. She shook her head, letting her hair fall across her face, as she lifted her hands to cover herself in the age-old gesture of modesty.

Alex said something softly, violently in his own language. His hands went round her and he lifted her on to the bed, tossing aside the coverlet but pulling the single sheet over her, hiding her.

Julia lay on her side, her whole body a curve of tension. Alex had gone round to the other side of the bed. Although she could not see him, she heard the faint rustle of his clothes as he removed them. She felt the mattress beside her dip under his weight, and her mind went blank with mingled fear and longing.

But he did not touch her, and when she evenutally dared a swift, furtive glance over her shoulder, it revealed that he was lying on his back as far from her as it was possible to get, his arms crossed behind his head as he stared at the ceiling.

Her throat contracted in sudden pain, and, almost involuntarily, the first scalding tears squeezed from beneath her eyelids and trickled slowly down her face. She caught her breath, then released it on a little trembling sigh.

She felt Alex move, lift himself up on his elbow.

He said, 'Julia?'

His hand took her shoulder, pulling her round to face him. For a long moment he looked at her, then gently he wiped the drops from her cheeks with his finger.

He said quietly, almost painfully, 'In all our time together, you have never wept until this moment.'

His arm went round her, pulling her against him, and her body went rigid, her hands bracing against the firm wall of his chest to push him away.

'Ah, Julia.' His voice was strained. 'Let me comfort you, if nothing else.'

He drew her to him, pillowing her head against his shoulder, his hand stroking the silky sheen of her hair, while she wept until there were no more tears left, then, still cradled against him, lulled by the beat of his heart, eventually she slept.

CHAPTER TEN

JULIA awoke early the next morning, her mind still programmed for Argoli.

Fetch the water, she thought, stretching, with a yawn, feed the hens . . . then paused, aware that her movement had not brought the usual creaking and groaning from the mattress.

Her eyes flew open, and with a gasp she registered her new surroundings, and the undoubted reality of Alex next to her, still asleep.

She turned her head and stared at the long naked curve of his back. Then, remembering her waking thoughts, she leaned across and shook him.

'Alex,' she said urgently. 'Alex!'

He groaned, and rolled to face her. His hair was tousled and he needed a shave, but her whole body clenched in longing at the sight of him.

'What is it?' he muttered. '*Christos*, it is barely dawn!'

'Penelope and the chickens,' she said. 'We left them behind on Argoli.'

'You've woken me to talk about goats and chickens?' He covered his eyes with his hand. 'May God give me patience!'

'But it's important,' Julia protested. 'They can't be left to starve—and Penelope will need milking . . .'

'All of them have been returned to their rightful

owners.' He sounded goaded beyond belief. 'Now may I have some peace?'

She said, 'Oh,' in a subdued voice, then, 'I'm sorry.'

'No more sorry than I, believe me.' He turned away again, punching the pillow into shape.

'Please don't be angry with me,' she said. 'I was worried . . .'

Alex threw her a glance of total incredulity over his shoulder.

'After everything that has happened, your only anxiety is a few animals? My God, now I've heard everything!'

'Oh, you're deliberately misunderstanding me!' Julia snapped angrily.

'I hope I am,' he returned grimly, and there was silence.

She put out a hand and touched his shoulder. The sensation of his cool, smooth skin under her fingers made her tremble. 'Alex—forgive me, please?'

He said, with a faint groan, 'Julia, go back to sleep.'

Her voice shook. 'Last night you held me.'

There was another pause. 'That was then,' he said, his words an ironic echo of her own. 'This is now.'

'Yes,' she said. 'This is now . . .'

She laid both palms flat on his shoulderblades, then bent forward, and with a catch of her breath kissed him where the dark hair grew low on the nape of his neck.

She felt the muscles in his back tense beneath her hands, then slowly he turned over and lay, facing her, his face expressionless. He put out a finger and smoothed an errant tress of hair behind her ear, then cupping his hand behind her head, he drew her towards him.

He began to kiss her, brushing his lips gently backwards and forwards across hers. For a while she lay passive, relishing the tenderness of the caress, resisting the urge to respond eagerly and carry it forward into a new dimension. But gradually the growing clamour of her flesh could not be denied, and she kissed him back, her lips parting, her tongue flickering heatedly against his.

He lifted his head at last and studied her for a long moment, holding her a little away from him. Then he tossed the tangled sheet away to the bottom of the bed and knelt, lifting her on to her knees in front of him.

Then he touched her slowly, his hands gliding with delicate sensuality over her breasts, down to her hips, and the swell of her buttocks to her flanks, then, softly and tinglingly, up her arching spine to her shoulders, repeating the movement over and over again, until every inch of skin, every nerve ending was pulsating in response. His fingers swooped to the silky triangle of hair between her thighs, touched her fleetingly, achingly, then left her again, to begin a whole new cycle of caresses.

Julia couldn't breathe. She couldn't even think coherently. She was aware of nothing but the wicked, tantalising sweep of his hands over her naked flesh, and the sweet, melting fire of need building inexorably inside her.

She tried to speak, but the only sound that escaped her taut throat was a little whimper of pure longing.

Alex said harshly, 'Yes, ah yes, *agapi mou.*' He

lifted her back against the pillows and came down against her, pinning her against the length of his hotly aroused body.

All control was gone, and there was no holding back any longer. Their mouths found each other, sucked and tore in frantic delight. Their hands moved in feverish, explicit demand.

She twisted against him, seeking him, and when he entered her she cried out sharply in pleasure. There was no pain this time, just a total completion, his body filling hers, making her one with him.

She clung to him, her nails raking his back and shoulders, her body moving with his in raw abandonment. Sunlight filled the room, and she was part of it, and so was he, and the pulse of her inner being seemed stronger than the universe as it met his. Caught in the heart of the sunburst, they were consumed, then flung out into some vast and dizzying void.

Afterwards there was silence. Reality returned slowly, and became Alex's arms still wrapped around her, Alex's head resting on her breasts. His weight against her was heaven, she thought, and holding him to her, she drifted into a sleep of sheer exhaustion.

The next time Julia awoke the bed beside her was empty. She lay for a moment, staring at the rumpled pillow, and remembering.

She must have been out for the count, she thought, blushing, because she hadn't been aware of Alex leaving, or of the fact that he had drawn the sheet up to cover her again.

She wondered what had woken her, and was alerted by a firm, slightly impatient knock on the bedroom door, which indicated that it might not have been the first.

'Er—come in,' she called, wriggling down in the bed and pulling the sheet to her chin.

The door opened to admit a plump, grey-haired woman, her black dress covered by a vast snowy apron. She was beaming with smiles, and carrying a tray laden with fruit juice, coffee, a selection of warm rolls and preserves, and several slices of honey cake.

She set the tray down beside Julia in the place which Alex had vacated, and burst into a flood of Greek. Julia looked at her in bewilderment, spreading her hands to convey her lack of comprehension, but nothing stemmed the torrent of words.

'Baraskevi.' Maria Xanthe, wearing a caftan in shades of peacock blue and gold, came into the room. She patted the older woman on the shoulder, speaking soothingly in her own language, and ushering her towards the door.

When it was safely closed behind her, she turned back smilingly to Julia. '*Kalimera*, little one. Baraskevi is my housekeeper here. I suppose Alex has told you all about her?'

Julia shook her head, horribly self-conscious about her lack of attire beneath the thin sheet, and also the fact that her nightdress was lying on the floor several feet away from the bed.

'No?' Maria Xanthe frowned. 'But that is astonishing—quite extraordinary! When he was a child, she was a second mother to him. He was born in her house on Argoli, and grew up as part of her family.'

'You mean the house we were living in—that Alex was repairing?'

Madame Xanthe's frown deepened. 'What are you saying? You used Baraskevi's house? Surely not? It has been empty longest, and is in a worse state than any of the others. The priest's house, for instance, is quite habitable, almost comfortable. Why didn't you stay there?'

Julia drank some fruit juice. 'Oh, I expect Alex had his reasons,' she said, trying to speak lightly. 'I—I thought from what he said that the house belonged to you.'

Maria Xanthe shook her head in bewilderment. 'Has he told you nothing then of his early life?' She sighed a little. 'I hoped that he would have spoken openly of it to you, his wife. Then I would know that he had forgiven me for sure.'

Forgiven her for what? Julia wondered, startled.

She said, 'Would you like some coffee? Baraskevi has brought two cups.'

Maria Xanthe shrugged. 'She thought Alex would still be with you, no doubt.'

'Do you know where he is?' Julia began to fill the cups.

'He took the car into Lymnos town a little while ago. Zoe has gone with him.'

Julia spilled some coffee on the tray. She said in a stifled voice, 'I see.'

'The island is quiet now,' Maria Xanthe went on, after a pause. 'But at the weekend things are different. Many people from Athens have villas here, and they come on the ferry. I have a number of friends among them.' She nodded. 'I shall give a party for you, *pedhi mou*. Introduce them all to my beautiful new daughter.'

'Oh, please, there's really no need,' Julia broke in, alarmed.

'But I love parties, and now I have a really good excuse.' Her mother-in-law patted her cheek. 'You cannot be shy, Julia *mou*, or unused to entertaining. I have seen pictures of your wonderful home in England, so you must be accustomed to welcoming guests.'

'Perhaps you should talk it over with Alex first,' Julia said desperately. 'You see, I—don't speak any Greek, which makes things difficult.'

Maria Xanthe laughed. 'Not with my friends. All of them speak English well,' she said. 'With Baraskevi there could be a problem. I shall have to interpret while she tells you about how beautiful Alex was when he was a baby, and how naughty as he grew older. She will also tell you how many candles she used to light for him in the church. She always said God listened specially to her prayers because she was born on Good Friday. That is what her name means—Friday. And now that he is safely married, to a beautiful wife, all her prayers have been answered.'

Julia spread some peach jam on a fragment of roll. 'I hope I don't disappoint her,' she said colourlessly. 'Wouldn't she have preferred him to marry a Greek girl?'

Maria Xanthe shrugged. 'Perhaps, but she knew in the end Alex would do just as he wanted.' She drank some of her coffee, looking preoccupied. 'But I

still cannot understand why Alex should have taken
you to that house. For me, naturally, it has
sentimental associations, but for a bride on her
honeymoon, *po po po!*'

Julia forced a smile. 'I wouldn't have thought it was
the ideal place to have a baby.'

The other woman laughed. 'Oh, that was not
intentional, *pedhi mou*. Let me explain. I was staying
here on Lymnos, waiting for my baby to be born. One
morning I felt—oh, restless. I wanted air, a breeze in
my face. So I persuaded Yannis to take me in his
caique to Argoli to visit his sister. He did not want
to—he tried to argue, but I would not listen. We had
hardly arrived at Baraskevi's house when without
warning my pains began. Two hours later Alex was
in my arms.' She sighed. 'But I was glad he was born
there. It was on Argoli that I had met George
Constantis. I was not famous then, you understand. I
was with a small Greek company which was making
a film using Argoli as location.'

She smiled reminiscently. 'I had a very tiny part in
this film, and he was an important man who had put
up some of the money for it. An old story, you might
think, but it was not so. We fell in love at first sight,
and although we were not fated to live our lives
together as we wished, we stayed in love.'

She took a slice of the honey cake. 'Was it like that
for you and my Alex? Did you know when you first
saw him that he would be the man for you?'

Julia said constrictedly, 'Not at once, perhaps, but
very soon. We—had a picnic by a lake, and we'd
quarrelled. I—I thought I would never see him again.
I felt wretched—empty as I walked home, and I

didn't understand why.' She thought silently, Maybe
I didn't want to understand . . .'

'Sometimes it is good to quarrel,' Madame Xanthe
said softly. 'Especially when making up can be so
sweet.'

Julia bent her head. 'I think Alex and I quarrel
rather too much,' she said stiltedly.

Madame laughed. 'Well, that is natural,' she said.
'Two strong personalities, learning to live together.'
She gave Julia's hair an amused tweak. 'And hair this
colour! Your lives together will never be dull.' She
drained her coffee and replaced the cup on the tray.
'You like to swim, Julia *mou*? Well, when you are
ready, join me by the pool.' She pulled a comic face.
'It is a way to escape from Thia Sophia's disapproval.
She does not care for the sun.' She gave Julia another
smile, and departed, tactfully ignoring the discarded
nightgown.

Julia made herself eat some more breakfast, then
went into the bathroom to shower, before putting on
a black and white bikini and a matching hip-length
jacket. She looked at herself in the long mirror and
gave a small sigh.

It had been a blow to waken after that passionate,
rapturous lovemaking and find that Alex was gone. It
was even more shattering to discover that he was
now with Zoe.

He couldn't have chosen a more emphatic way of
showing her how little their coming together had
meant to him, she thought with painful bitterness.
What a fool she'd been to think their physical
attunement could possibly affect the future of their
relationship! To Alex, it had just been sex, a way of

ridding himself of frustration, but unimportant in the long term.

He had married her for all the wrong reasons, she thought miserably, and was now totally intent on freeing himself from the disastrous result of his impulse.

She turned away, biting her lip. Even without Tricia Bosworth's malevolent intervention she would still have found it difficult to convince Alex that her early hostility to him had been fuelled by a complexity of emotions she had been too inexperienced to analyse or express.

And now it was too late.

That silly fantasy about living alone at Ambermere, her own mistress, was all set to come true, just when she had realised it was the last thing in the world that she wanted.

It wasn't the easiest morning Julia had ever spent. Maria Xanthe's warmth and friendliness to which, in other circumstances, Julia would have joyfully responded, was yet another pitfall. There were so many topics of conversation to be avoided, so many no-go areas, she realised ruefully.

Paul Constantis had also decided to spend the morning beside the pool, which created additional difficulties. Julia was aware that he was listening avidly to everything that was said, and found this disturbing. Madame Xanthe might have arranged a reconciliation with the rest of the family, but Julia wasn't convinced this went deeper than the surface. Paul, she was sure, would seize any opportunity to damage Alex if he could, and this meant she had to be doubly careful when Madame Xanthe referred yet again to their honeymoon on Argoli.

Alex and Zoe returned shortly before lunch was served, the other girl hanging possessively to his arm, wreathed in smiles.

Sick at heart, Julia looked away, wondering what Alex had been saying to his cousin to light her up like that. Had he hinted, she wondered, at what the future might hold? If so, then the sooner she left Lymnos the better. Every giggle from Zoe, every flutter of her eyelashes was like a knife turning in her heart.

Murmuring something about the heat of the sun, she swung herself off her lounger and started back to the villa.

Before she had got even half-way, a hand fell on her shoulder, and Alex's voice said sharply, 'Julia, wait!'

She turned reluctantly to face him, thankful for the sunglasses that masked her eyes. 'Yes?'

'We must talk.'

'I thought everything had already been said.' A small, fragile hope began to burgeon inside her.

His face was taut, his mouth grimly set, as he looked at her. 'I owe you an apology. I—should not have imposed my presence on you last night, as I did. If I'd used another room, then—this morning—could not have happened. I offer my profound regrets, and my assurance that it will not occur again.'

The hope withered and died. Julia said with an effort, 'Thank you, but you don't have to apologise. It—it was my fault too.' She paused. 'I—I think I should cut my visit here as short as possible.' She tried to smile. 'Your mother is talking of giving a party for me.'

Alex mouth tightened. 'I will deal with it,' he said abruptly, and turned away.

Just a minor problem, thought Julia, watching him go. And ridding himself of an unwanted wife would only be another one.

She sighed soundlessly and went back to the house.

Julia stood by the tall windows of the *saloni*, staring listlessly across the gardens. In the ten days since Alex had brought her to Lymnos, this room had become very much her refuge. She usually retreated to it in the afternoons, so that she didn't have to see Alex and Zoe together.

Everywhere she went was where they seemed to be, she thought bitterly. If she was down beside the pool, Zoe would be there displaying her admittedly gorgeous figure in a series of ever more minuscule bikinis. If she went to the bay, Alex would be teaching Zoe to windsurf, or they would be water-skiing. At first Paul had been with them too, but now they made no pretence of needing anyone else's company but their own.

Julia had been offered her turn on the windsurfer, and behind the speedboat, but it was clear that the suggestion had been polite and perfunctory, and once she had refused, it was not made again.

Why doesn't he let me go? she asked herself wearily. Why does he keep me here, enduring this?

One of the worst times had been when it had become obvious that Alex was occupying a separate bedroom. It was, she had realised helplessly, impossible to keep such an arrangement private.

Maria Xanthe had been openly distressed about it, and even Thia Sophia had delivered herself, over dinner one night, of a majestic and largely incomprehensible lecture on the duties of a wife to her husband.

Sheer hypocrisy, Julia thought tiredly. The old witch must be secretly delighted about it all. She certainly never failed to beam approving glances at her daughter when she flirted outrageously with Alex.

'So here you are,' said a voice, and Julia half turned to see Paul watching her, his eyes frankly speculative.

'Well spotted,' she returned drily.

He laughed, and came to stand beside her. 'I've missed you these past few days,' he remarked. 'My leave will be over soon, and I have to get back to the Embassy.' He paused, then said almost idly, 'Why don't you come with me?'

Julia jumped. She said coolly, 'You seem to forget I'm married.'

'I forget nothing Julia *mou*. It is my cousin Alex who seems to have difficulty with his memory.' His hand began to stroke her arm. 'I cannot bear to see how he neglects you,' he whispered.

Julia stepped firmly out of range of his caressing fingers. 'Please don't concern yourself,' she said crisply. 'Alex and I—understand each other very well.'

His brows lifted. 'Every wife should be so sympathetic! Or is it perhaps that you just don't care?

You are very beautiful, Julia, but it takes more than beauty to warm a man's bed. Does your bridegroom not please you—or are you frigid, perhaps?' He took a step towards her, smiling. 'That was not the impression I got during our evening together. You should have married me, Julia *mou*, not my cousin Alex's money. I could melt you . . .'

'How dare you!' Julia took another step back, to find herself against the wall. 'I hope you know that you're making an utter fool of yourself.'

'Am I?' he murmured. 'Well, let us see . . .'

He reached for her, his mouth fastening on hers, his tongue trying to force its way between her tightly closed lips. Julia braced her hands against his chest, trying desperately to push him away, and when that didn't work she kicked him as hard as she could on the shin.

Paul let her go, cursing, and she ran behind one of the sofas. 'Get out of here!' she told him breathlessly.

'Little wildcat,' he said, half laughing, half angry. 'I should have taken you while I had the chance!'

'You never had the chance,' Julia said icily. 'Don't come near me again, unless you want me to tell Alex.'

'Do you think he would care?' Paul shook his head. 'His whole attitude tells the world he has made a mistake which he regrets. Cut your losses, Julia *mou*. Come with me.'

'Not if you were the last man alive!'

He shrugged. 'Then you are destined to be very much alone, I think.' He gave her a nonchalant look and walked to the door.

Julia sank down on to the sofa, wiping her mouth

violently with the back of her hand.

She thought, trembling, I can't take any more of this. I've got to get away from here. I've got to . . .

CHAPTER ELEVEN

'YOU ARE leaving?' Maria Xanthe asked in astonishment. 'But Alex has said nothing!'

A myriad excuses and explanations, each more feeble than the last, chased through Julia's mind and were discarded.

She said quietly, 'Alex doesn't know. 'I—I'm going alone, Madame Xanthe.'

There was silence, then Maria Xanthe gave a deep sigh. 'I—see. Well, it was evident that all was not well between you, *pedhi mou*, but is it really necessary to leave—to give up? Whatever Alex has done, could you not find it in your heart to give him a second chance?'

Julia gave her a startled look, 'No, you don't understand. It's Alex who wants to be rid of me.' She bent her head. 'From the moment we met, I behaved badly, you see—said some stupid things. Alex only married me to—punish me for them.'

'What are you saying?' The older woman looked appalled. 'To marry for such a reason! No one would do such a thing. You have misunderstood, my child.'

'I only wish I had.' Julia bit her lip. 'You thought Alex had taken me to Argoli out of sentiment.' She shook her head. 'It was to teach me a lesson. I—I called him a peasant, and he decided to show me

171

what a peasant's life was like, the hard way, by making me work from sunrise to sunset.' She swallowed. 'He also made it clear that he didn't intend the marriage to be a—a real one.'

Maria Xanthe said shrewdly, 'But about that, he changed his mind?'

'Yes—eventually.'

'Oh, my poor children!' Maria made a gesture of appeal to the heavens. 'No wonder you both look so bruised! That there are so many silences between you.' She gave Julia a straight look. 'You love my Alex?'

'Yes,' Julia admitted sadly. 'But he doesn't know that—and he wouldn't believe it either. He thinks I married him just so that I can go on living in my family home.'

'That beautiful English house that he has bought? I wondered about the reason for that. Doesn't it seem to you, *pedhi mou*, that he must care for you a great deal to do this thing for you?'

Julia shook her head. 'He'd decided to buy Ambermere before he'd even met me. Later he discovered—how much the house meant to me, and as he—needed a wife, it seemed a convenient arrangement.'

Maria Xanthe snorted. 'Needed a wife! What nonsense is this? Alex has been fighting to stay single for the past ten years. Then suddenly—so suddenly, he telephones and says that he is going to be married to an English girl with hair like flame. He said nothing of any—arrangement.' She made the word sound like a blasphemy, and in spite of her unhappiness Julia found herself smiling.

'So first this marriage was for punishment. Now it is for convenience,' Maria went on, after a pause. 'Which is the true reason, I wonder? Or is it neither of them?'

'I no longer know what to think,' Julia returned wearily. 'It's all such a hopeless—mess.' She gave a little sigh. 'I can't blame Alex for wanting to cut his losses and be free. In fact, I don't blame him for anything.' She flushed slightly. 'I really was an appalling little snob. I—I needed a lesson.'

'Perhaps,' Maria Xanthe shrugged. 'But my son's methods seem a little drastic. Even so, you are a beautiful girl, Julia *mou*, and a passionate one, I think. Could you have not found some way to convince Alex that he was wrong, that he meant more to you than—this house?'

'I hoped I could,' said Julia, in a low voice. 'But I failed there too.' Briefly, she outlined Tricia Bosworth's intervention and its consequences. 'So you see, Alex had every reason to feel—betrayed.'

'Ah, yes.' Maria Xanthe sighed deeply. 'And not for the first time, *pedhi mou*. I have my own share of guilt in all this.'

'You have? I don't understand . . .'

'When I found I was to have my George's child, I was not ashamed, you understand, because I loved him. But I was frightened. Times were different then. People were not so—understanding. The fact that I had an illegitimate child could have damaged my career.' She paused. 'Alex was only a few weeks old when my agent contacted me to tell me the results of a screen test I'd had for a Hollywood studio. The news was good—they wanted me. But they wanted someone fresh, without encumbrances, without a past.'

She clasped her hands together in her lap. 'Baraskevi was childless, and she had cared devotedly for Alex and myself when he was born. Gradually I convinced myself that the baby would be better off if he stayed with her. If he was brought up on Argoli simply and healthily, rather than being ''a film star's child'', dragged round in my wake from location to location. I told myself I was doing it for him, all for him. Maybe I even believed it,' she added with a grimace.

'But it wasn't true?' Julia stared at her.

'In part, I think so, yes. Nothing about Hollywood ever suggested it was a good environment for bringing up a child. So Alex grew up, miles away, an island child, thinking Baraskevi was his mother.'

'Did you never see him?'

'I saw him often. Sometimes, if George could get away, he came with me. But we were visitors, nothing more, to him. Honoured guests.' She smiled sadly. 'When George decided to make Alex his heir, he had to be told the truth.'

'And how did he take it?'

'He was hurt badly. At first he did not believe it, then he became very angry. He accused me of being ashamed of him, of rejecting him for my own selfish reasons. For a long time he would not look at me or speak to me. And like you, *pedhi mou*, I could not blame him for his bitterness. In those early days I was ambitious. I did not want a scandal. But I had been punished too. There was not a day that I did not think about my son, and long to have him near me.'

'But he did forgive you.'

'Eventually, yes. But it was not easy. I had to break down the hurt—the resentment—prove to Alex over and over again that I loved him, that I would never reject him again. Slowly he began to trust me—to care in return. We developed a relationship, and now things are good between us, although it is still not generally known that I am his mother, even now. The family know, and the lawyers, but few others. And now that I live in retirement my activities are no longer of such great interest to the newspapers.' She patted Julia's cheek. 'But I am still careful. You may have wondered why I did not come to the wedding, for example.

'But—and I blame myself for this—the past has made Alex wary too. He has always taken his pleasure lightly—reluctant to commit himself deeply to a woman. I had begun to think he would never marry.' She paused, then said gently, 'If he had reason to believe you did not love him, Julia *mou*, it could explain why he has been so harsh with you—so unforgiving. For him, perhaps love has come to mean—betrayal.'

She put a hand over Julia's. 'And he did love you, little one. When he spoke to me of you, it sang in his voice, in his words, and I was so happy for him, so thankful that I cried with joy.' She shook her head. 'These last few days—seeing the separation between you, the coldness—have almost broken my heart.'

'And mine,' Julia whispered, and Madame Xanthe put her arms round her and hugged her fiercely.

'So—what is to be done?'

'Alex wants a divorce,' Julia said simply. 'He intends to marry his cousin Zoe.'

Madame Xanthe grimaced. 'That is a joke,' she said grimly. 'Only not funny. She would bore him in a week, that one.'

'But that doesn't alter the fact that he's been paying her a lot of attention.'

'And because of this, you intend to run away. What answer is that?'

'The only one I can think of.' Julia's hands twisted together in her lap. 'I need to think—get things into perspective. Here, I'm too close to it all.' She lifted her chin. 'I'd like to catch the evening ferry to Piraeus.'

'Ah, no.' Madame Xanthe shook her head. 'If you are determined to go, then at least I insist that Yannis takes you in our own boat in comfort.'

'Thank you.' Julia hesitated. 'Actually, I was going to ask if I could—borrow Yannis for a while today. There's something I want to do, something I want to see again before I go.'

'I think I can guess.' Maria Xanthe's eyes were misty. 'Yannis is at your service, little one. Just tell him at what time you wish to leave.' She paused. 'Are you going to say goodbye to Alex?'

'He's taken Zoe sailing for the day.' Julia's teeth sank painfully into her lower lip. 'I've written him a letter.'

'I see,' Maria Xanthe said heavily. 'I wish it could all have been different for you, *pedhi mou*. You are the daughter I always wanted.'

Julia hugged her in turn. 'I shall miss you too,' she whispered.

Argoli was languid in the afternoon heat as Julia walked slowly up the village street. No breeze stirred the silver of the olive trees today, and the only sound was the buzz of the unseen cicadas.

She had arranged with much careful sign language for Yanni to return for her in three hours, and then he would take her straight to Piraeus. Once in Athens she would find a hotel for the night, and hope to get a scheduled flight the following day back to England.

But first she had had to come back here—to the place where the brief drama of her marriage had been played out, half comedy, half tragedy.

When she reached Baraskevi's house she stopped and took a long look at it. Alex's renovations and repairs had made an amazing difference, she thought, running a finger along the edge of one of the new window-frames. And there was plenty of land at the back for the house to extend into, if only . . .

She stopped herself abruptly. There was no future in that kind of thinking, those kind of regrets.

Now she had to rely on the letter she had left for Alex. Such a slender foundation on which to build her hopes, but it was all she had.

In my own way, I'm as much a gambler as my father, she thought. But the stakes are even higher. I've got my happiness, my whole life on the line.

She went into the house. Even after a few days the living-room had a wistful, neglected look, and dust was beginning to gather on the surfaces.

She wondered if Alex's plans for the islanders' return would succeed, and if he would ever use this house again himself. Maria Xanthe had been brutally honest about her motives for leaving him here, but on the other hand, Julia could think of few better places for a young child growing up.

Her remark to Paul about the possibility of using the house as a holiday retreat had been made on the spur of the moment, but it was still a wonderful idea, or would have been under other circumstances. Perhaps Alex would still bring his children here, she thought with a pang, although she couldn't see the sybaritic Zoe warming to conditions here.

But there was no denying that Alex had been safe and loved on Argoli, even though the subsequent discovery that his secure world was built upon deception must have been a terrible blow to him.

She sighed. No wonder Alex was as he was! That vulnerability she had sensed went deeper than she could ever have guessed. Not even Baraskevi's devotion could have shielded him from the fact that his mother had virtually abandoned him, she thought sadly. That knowledge must have made him question the value of his very existence.

And I've just made everything worse, she thought.

Looking back on the short period before they were married, Julia could see that there had been endless opportunities then to tell Alex—to show him incontrovertibly that she loved him. She could have

broken down the formal barriers that he had imposed
on their courtship and brought warmth and life to it.
On their wedding day, they should have been so
close that nothing and no one, least of all Tricia
Bosworth, could have come between them. Together
they could have laughed away her pathetic barbs.

But pride had still been a factor then, and that, and
her uncertainty about his feelings for her, had kept
her silent and aloof. So, instead of the reassurance he
needed from her, Alex had received chilling evidence
that she was just as mercenary, just as scathing
towards him as he could have feared.

Slowly Julia climbed the wooden stairway to the
upper room and stood looking round her. It was just
as she had left it, except the green dress was no
longer on the floor beside the bed where she had
dropped it. Nor was it in the chest. In fact, to her
absurd disappointment, it had completely vanished.

And she had wanted it. One of the reasons for
coming here had been to get it, to take it back to
England with her. It was a link with the past, a signal
reminder of that brief time here with Alex—probably
the only one she would ever have.

There was no guarantee, after all, that he would
even read her letter, let alone believe any of the
things she had said in it. He might well feel so
relieved about her departure that he would consign
her letter to the waste basket, and herself to some
kind of mental limbo.

With a little sigh she went downstairs and out into
the sunlight, standing irresolutely for a minute.
Perhaps it had been a mistake to come here. She
would have done better to bypass Argoli altogether,

and got Yannis to take her straight to Piraeus without sentimental detours for souvenirs that didn't exist, reviving memories which could only bring her pain.

In the meantime, she had another couple of hours to kill. I'll go and get some water from the spring, she thought, then go to the beach.

She took an empty bottle from one of the cupboards and rinsed it again and again under the cold, sparkling water, before filling it to the brim.

She walked back down the track, between the gnarled trunks of the olive trees, past the spot where Penelope had been tethered, and back into the full glare of the sunlight.

He was standing a few yards away, watching her, and at the sight of him, so unexpected, so sharply, poignantly beloved, Julia cried out, and the bottle of water fell from her hands and smashed on the stony ground at her feet.

He said hoarsely, 'I was on my boat, and I saw Yannis leaving here. I wondered . . .' He swallowed, and Julia saw his hands clench into fists at his sides. 'What are you doing here?'

'I came for one last look. When Yannis comes presently, he's taking me to Piraeus.'

Alex drew a breath. 'You are going?' he demanded. 'Without a word to me?'

'I thought everything had already been said.' Julia moistened her lips with the tip of her tongue. 'And I have—written to you. The letter's in your room at the villa.'

He smiled bitterly. 'Thank you for that, at least.'

The dark eyes swept over her from the top of her head to the soles of her sandalled feet. He said, half to himself, 'So this is how it ends.'

'I thought a clean break was best,' she said. 'Particularly . . .' She stopped.

'What were you going to say?'

'Oh, that everyone knows the situation between us—and it's becoming embarrassing.' She tried to smile. 'Your cousin Paul seems to think I need—consolation.'

'And do you?'

'Not from him.'

'Yet you knew him first.'

'I met him,' she corrected.

'And, from that meeting, got your original impressions of me.' The dark gaze held hers. 'They were important, I think.'

'But it's the last ones I shall remember,' Julia said huskily, and there was a silence. She added, 'Don't let me keep you from your sailing. Zoe will be wondering where you are.'

'She is not with me. She complained, as usual, that the wind was spoiling her hair, and the spray was ruining her clothes. So I restored her safely to dry land, and her doting mother.' Alex laughed harshly. 'I don't think water is her favourite element, but it has been—almost amusing to see what lengths she has been prepared to go to in order to impress me during this week.'

Julia bit her lip. 'That's not very kind of you.'

'But I am not always kind,' he said. 'As who should know better than you, *matia mou?*'

Julia looked down at the ground. 'I—I'd better clear up this broken glass. If you're going to have other animals here . . .'

'There will be nothing,' he said bleakly. 'I shall not come here again.'

'You're going to waste all that hard work on the house?'

'It is already wasted.' He shrugged. 'But why should you care, Julia *mou*, about a peasant's hovel on a remote island? You are going home to your beloved Ambermere. You will soon forget this place, and everything about it.'

'I wish I could believe that. And the letter I wrote you concerns Ambermere.'

Alex frowned. 'I have already told you that I will give it to you when we are divorced. I will not go back on my word.'

'I'm sure you won't.' Julia lifted her chin. 'Actually, what I want is your permission to sell it.'

'You wish to—sell Ambermere—your home?' The dark face was incredulous. 'What are you talking about? Have you gone mad?'

'No,' she said quietly. 'I think I've managed to become sane at last.' She swallowed. 'You talk about Ambermere being my home, but if I have to live there alone, it's nothing but an empty shell. It means nothing—nothing at all. And that's what I wrote to you in my letter.'

'Why should you tell me such a thing?' His voice was rough. His eyes seemed to bore into her face.

For a moment Julia's courage almost failed her, and then she remembered Maria Xanthe's words, 'I had to break down the hurt—the resentment.' Now was her chance. Could she really do less?

She took a step towards him. Her voice quivered. 'Because I thought if Ambermere was no longer there, clouding the issue, you might believe me if I said I loved you.'

Alex was very white under his deep tan. 'Julia, be careful what you are saying. Don't joke with me.'

'I was never more serious,' she told him passionately. 'What more can I do or say to prove it? I love you, Alex, and I want you and I need you. You set out to humble my pride. Well, I've none left where you're concerned.' She gestured round her. 'What do you think I'm doing here now, but thinking—and remembering? I tried to hate you for all that you put me through, but instead I ended up loving you more than ever.'

She gave a little choky laugh. 'I came back to look for that grotty green dress you made me wear, so that I would have something—tangible to remember you by. Only it's gone. I don't even have that any more.'

He said hoarsely, 'I can tell you where it is. It's in my room at the villa, under my pillow. It was all I had of you, *agapi mou*. I kept telling myself that it was all that I deserved to have, after the way I had treated you.'

Julia said shakily, 'I asked for it—every little bit. Oh, Alex—*Alex* . . .'

He took a quick stride towards her and pulled her roughly into his arms. His mouth took hers in a kiss of aching, passionate tenderness, and his hands held her as if he would never let her go.

When they drew apart, they were both trembling.

Alex said huskily, 'I have dreamed so often of you telling me that you loved me, my beautiful one. Now it is true at last.'

'It's been true for a long time.' Julia stroked his cheek, and ran a caressing forefinger across his lips. 'I would have told you that the first night on board the *Clio*, but I didn't get the chance. And you wouldn't have believed me anyway,' she added gently.

'Forgive me.' Alex took her back into the shelter of his arms. 'I accused you of pride, Julia *mou*, yet it was my own pride that was hurt. I wanted to lash back at you, make you suffer as I had done. But when I made you sorry, it gave me no satisfaction. You were so brave about it all.' He put his lips against her forehead.

She gave him a teasing smile. 'When I'd recovered from the first shock, it was quite a challenge!'

'Can you forget it ever happened, my sweet one?' Alex's voice was urgent, pleading. 'Can we wipe out the last miserable weeks, and pretend that our marriage begins now at this moment?'

'Well—we could.' Julia smiled up at him, sliding her arms round his neck. 'But there are certain things that happened here that I'd quite like to remember.'

His brows rose quizzically. 'Indeed?'

'Why, yes,' she said. 'I actually learned to make edible bread. And I managed to milk Penelope. Real achievements, those.'

'They must have been,' he murmured gravely. He bent his head and kissed her slowly, and very thoroughly. 'Is there nothing else you recall, hmm?'

'I seem to have a dim recollection,' Julia said demurely, and gasped as Alex swung her off her feet and up into his arms. 'What are you doing?'

'Jogging your memory, *matia mou.*' He grinned down at her wickedly. 'Which of us has the better mattress, I wonder? I know, we'll try them both.'

They came together in laughter which was all the sweeter for the pain which had preceded it. They undressed each other between kisses, murmuring the words of love so long withheld, their bodies joining with a hunger which would not be denied, both giving without limit, reaching the sharp agonised delight of fulfilment together.

A long time later Julia said drowsily, 'We'll have to get a bigger bed.'

'Will we?' Alex lifted his head from the scented pillow of her breasts and smiled at her. 'There is a bigger bed at the villa.'

'But it isn't here,' she objected. She paused. 'Besides, we'd have to face Thia Sophia, and she won't be pleased to find that you aren't marrying Zoe after all.'

He grinned sardonically. 'But Zoe will be more than relieved I think. I drove her hard, lost my temper with her more than once, *matia mou*, while I was trying to make you jealous. Did I succeed?'

'Only too well,' Julia admitted with a little sigh. 'Poor Zoe!'

'Not to mention her brother,' remarked Alex, between his teeth. 'So he wished to console you. I must remember to thank him for his kindness.'

'I already have,' Julia confessed. 'His shin may well

be scarred for life.'

'And so may my back,' muttered Alex, easing his shoulders. 'Wildcat!'

'I'm sorry,' she said remorsefully.

'I'm not.' He kissed her, biting softly at her lower lip. 'You are the woman of my dreams and more, *eros mou.*'

'Then why did you move to another room at your mother's house?'

'Because I was ashamed of wanting you—of forcing myself on a woman who didn't care for me. Of behaving like—some Greek stud.' He put his finger on her lips, silencing the protest she was about to make. 'Oh, yes, I could make you want me in return, but I needed so much more from you than just a response.' He kissed her again. 'And now I have it.'

She began to touch him, sliding her hands over his body, revelling in her freedom to do so.

'Darling, do we have to go back to Lymnos? Couldn't we arrange for some supplies, and stay here by ourselves?'

'You'd be more comfortable at the villa,' muttered Alex, groaning pleasurably at the caress of her fingers. 'Getting a bigger bed here will take time.'

'But we've got time,' Julia said eagerly. 'And there's lots more work to do on this house. Another room at the back would be nice.' She stroked the dark hair back from his forehead. 'We'll need more space, when the children come.'

'Our children,' Alex said with a short sigh of contentment. 'Conceived here, and born at

Ambermere. How does that sound, *agapi mou?*'

'It sounds wonderful—but Alex, I meant what I said. You can sell the house, if you want.'

He shook his head. 'I don't want. I love the house, and I love you, my beautiful girl, and we are going to live at Ambermere and be happy.'

She said softly, 'It doesn't matter where we live, as long as we're together. Oh, Alex, I love you so much!'

'And I love you, my wife, to my life's end, and beyond.'

'To my life's end and beyond,' she echoed, and drew him down to her once more.

A WORLD WHERE PASSION AND DESIRE ARE FUSED

CRYSTAL FLAME — *Jayne Ann Krentz* _____ £2.95
He was fire — she was ice — together their passion was a crystal flame. An exceptional story entwining romance with the excitement of fantasy.

PINECONES AND ORCHIDS — *Suzanne Ellison* _____ £2.50
Tension and emotion lie just below the surface in this outstanding novel of love and loyalty.

BY ANY OTHER NAME — *Jeanne Triner* _____ £2.50
Money, charm, sophistication, Whitney had it all, so why return to her past? The mystery that surrounds her is revealed in this moving romance.

These three new titles will be out in bookshops from October 1988.

W❂RLDWIDE

 **ROMANCE**

Next month's romances from Mills & Boon

Each month, you can choose from a world of variety in romance with Mills & Boon. These are the new titles to look out for next month.

THE RIGHT MAN Sandra Field
NO WAY TO SAY GOODBYE Kay Gregory
HIGHLAND TURMOIL Stephanie Howard
WITHOUT TRUST Penny Jordan
A PRICELESS LOVE Emma Darcy
JUST A NORMAL MARRIAGE Leigh Michaels
MAN WITHOUT A PAST Valerie Parv
WHEN THE LOVING STOPPED Jessica Steele
WHEN THE GODS CHOOSE Patricia Wilson
NO GENTLE LOVING Sara Wood
LOVE BY DEGREE Debbie Macomber
BUT NEVER LOVE Lynsey Stevens
A TAMING HAND Jenny Arden
HEIRS TO LOVING Rachel Ford

Buy them from your usual paperback stockist, or write to: Mills & Boon Reader Service, P.O. Box 236, Thornton Rd, Croydon, Surrey CR9 3RU, England. Readers in Southern Africa — write to: Independent Book Services Pty, Postbag X3010, Randburg, 2125, S. Africa.

Mills & Boon
the rose of romance

Mills & Boon

AND THEN HE KISSED HER...

This is the title of our new venture — an audio tape designed to help you become a successful Mills & Boon author!

In the past, those of you who asked us for advice on how to write for Mills & Boon have been supplied with brief printed guidelines. Our new tape expands on these and, by carefully chosen examples, shows you how to make your story come alive. And we think you'll enjoy listening to it.

You can still get the printed guidelines by writing to our Editorial Department. But, if you would like to have the tape, please send a cheque or postal order for £4.95 (which includes VAT and postage) to:

VAT REG. No. 232 4334 96

AND THEN HE KISSED HER...

To: Mills & Boon Reader Service, FREEPOST, P.O. Box 236, Croydon, Surrey CR9 9EL.

Please send me _____ copies of the audio tape. I enclose a cheque/postal order*, crossed and made payable to Mills & Boon Reader Service, for the sum of £_____. *Please delete whichever is not applicable.

Signature _____

Name (BLOCK LETTERS) _____

Address _____

_____ Post Code _____

YOU MAY BE MAILED WITH OTHER OFFERS AS A RESULT OF THIS APPLICATION   ED1